$\mathcal{P}$LAYING *for* $\mathcal{K}$EEPS

G★ME
Changers

A.C. ARTHUR

An Artistry Publishing Book
PLAYING FOR KEEPS, First Edition: 2020
Copyright © 2020 by A.C. Arthur
All rights reserved.
Cover Art Design © 2020 by Croco Designs

This book is a work of fiction. Characters, names, locations, events and incidents (in either a contemporary and/or historical setting) are products of the author's imagination and are being used in an imaginative manner as a part of this work of fiction. Any resemblance to actual events, locations, settings or persons, living or dead, is entirely coincidental.

www.acarthur.net

1

*G*CSports18: Tell me what you like.

Rylan stared at her phone screen; fingers poised to type a response.

She didn't know what to say. Or rather she did, she just wondered if she *should* say it. After all, she had no idea who GCSports18 was. He'd popped up on the social networking site she was using to livestream karaoke night at the Game Changers Sports Bar & Grill.

Karaoke wasn't usually her thing, but tonight was a special occasion. Ethan Henley, who co-owned the bar with five of his close friends and had grown up here in Providence, Virginia along with Rylan, was getting married on New Year's Day. His fiancé, Portia Merin, was also from Providence but she'd gone away to college and came back as an intimacy instructor. With Thanksgiving, Christmas and the weeks Portia had to travel for work coming up, Rylan's best friend and Portia's maid of honor, Camelia "Camy" Greer decided to throw Portia's bachelorette party a little early. The second week of November was probably a lot early, but the group of six women were having a fantastic time on this rainy Friday evening.

GCSports18 commented on the show and the rousing rendition of Aretha Franklin's *Respect* by Kasey, one of the waitresses that worked at the bar. Rylan replied in agreement that Kasey was rockin' the house with her sassy attitude and stage presence. After a few more comments that Rylan barely recalled because she was simultaneously chatting with others who were responding to her video, GCSports18's screen name and bullseye icon appeared in a dropdown on her screen. It was a private message. Rylan had no idea who this person was or when they'd connected on the site. She didn't normally spend time online. Managing and working on vehicles at Kent Automotive took up a lot of her time. She wasn't certain that would be the case by the end of this year, but Rylan was determined not to think about that tonight. The staggered private conversation with GCSports18 had been going on for about twenty minutes, during which time she'd surmised he was a guy after he'd mentioned playing pool at an all boys' club when he was a kid. She'd responded to his comment about the boys' club with a comment about her early-sprouting breasts keeping her out of boys' activities since she was eight years old. It was after that comment that Rylan sensed their conversation taking a very sexual tone.

"I'm going to advise you ladies go lightly on this next pitcher of Pink Panty Dropper. Despite what I'm sure would be the pleasure of more than one guy in the crowd, absolutely no panties will be dropped in Game Changers tonight. Or any other night, for that matter," Delano "Del" Greer, part owner and manager of the bar, spoke in his deep somber voice, his lips barely lifting in what she knew was his general pass for a smile.

Rylan had known Del for the majority of her life, since she'd met Camy at Ms. Anne's daycare when they were five years old. Camy was Del's younger sister. Del and his twin brother

Delancey, who they called Lance, were three years older than Camy and Rylan.

Camy laughed and clapped a hand on Del's shoulder. He was a little over six feet tall, but Camy was sitting in a high-boy chair so they were almost face-to-face.

"You just head on back over there to the bar where you've been standing and stewing all night, big brother," Camy said before rubbing her fingers over the side of the pitcher filled with the pretty pink beverage. "And we'll continue to enjoy ourselves at this lovely party."

Camy's light brown eyes were a little glazed and her smile was constant. Rylan

knew what that meant. She would definitely be tonight's designated driver. With that thought, she figured she might as well finish off the first drink she'd had tonight. The Pink Panty Dropper packed a hell of a punch, but she'd enjoyed a perfectly cooked well-done filet at Milligan's Steakhouse, where the bachelorette party had started earlier tonight.

"I think somebody over there might like it if my panties get dropped," Portia said between the giggles she'd had for the last half hour.

"I hear that!" Brenda Cole, who went to school with Camy and Rylan, said before lifting her empty glass into the air to toast with whoever thought what she'd said was a good idea.

Gina Rivera, who taught Zumba classes at the gym, lifted her glass to clink loudly with Brenda's and Rylan grinned while shaking her head because Del didn't find any of that funny.

"My fiancé is over there working, Del. And I happen to know for a fact that he prefers me panty-less," Portia continued.

Now Del pinched the bridge of his nose and closed his eyes. This was a familiar reaction too. Unlike Lance who would've most likely laughed and provided a quick and raunchy retort, Del probably felt uncomfortable considering Ethan was one of his best friends.

"Not here," Del said when he opened his eyes again. "This is the last pitcher for you ladies. Only coffee after this."

His tone was stern and he topped it off by giving a curt nod, his medium-thick lips drawn tight, a muscle twitching in his jaw. Rylan didn't actually see that muscle twitch because of Del's full beard. But she knew it was there because it always appeared when he was agitated or worried. She knew Del like he was the brother she never had.

And because that was a fact, the moment he walked away from the table, Rylan looked at her phone screen once again. GCSports18 was still waiting for her response. She should close out of the app and put her phone in her purse. Nothing was going to come of an oddly sexual chat session with a stranger. Not for her anyway. While Portia and Ethan may be blissfully in love, Rylan was currently witnessing the divorce from hell play out between her parents.

Rylan: I'm not into roses and candlelight.

She typed because one of her mother's chief complaints about her father was that he didn't wine and dine her enough.

Estelle Kent had a list of complaints against Will, her husband of thirty-seven years, that was easily longer than Rylan's left arm…and her right leg. Which was precisely why Rylan had no intention of ever getting married or even giving her heart to a man. But this was only chatting. While she hadn't been on a date in almost three months, Rylan wasn't yet ready to venture into online dating. And if she ever considered it, she definitely wouldn't start the conversation while drinking at a bachelorette party. That was a sure recipe for disaster.

Del hated social media.

He despised the idea of putting his personal business online for billions of strangers to dissect and devour. He also didn't like the amount of time it took out of the lives of a good majority of the people in this world on a daily basis.

But Noah Jordan—one of his closest friends and the marketing guru of Game Changers —could be as big a nag as anyone that Del had ever had the displeasure of meeting in his thirty-one years of life.

"Great crowd tonight," Ethan, the bartender, said when Del once again joined him behind the bar.

The Brothers—as they used to call themselves—Del, Ethan, Noah, Rochester "Rock" Patterson, Jeret McCoy and Del's twin brother Delancey "Lance" had been as close as if they were all blood-related since the time they'd spent together as teens at the Grace House for Boys.

"Yeah," Del replied and looked out to the main floor to see that almost all of their tables were full of guests.

The Bullpen area, which was where he'd just come from, tending to Ethan's fiancé's bachelorette party, was also full. Upstairs, the private area they called the Skybox had been reserved by one of the bowling leagues attending an annual conference at the Regional Resort and Spa in Alexandria. Drinks were flowing, food was being brought out of the kitchen in regular intervals and the entertainment that Lance insisted would be a success was certainly entertaining the crowd. Del was happy. Even if it didn't look like it.

They were closing in ninety minutes. An hour after that, Del and the brothers, along with their staff, would finish cleaning up the place and head to their respective homes. Del planned to grab a hot shower and fall face first into his bed. But before any of that happened, he would have to do something he hated. And not because he thought he was above doing it, but because he hated the smirk he knew he was going to see on Noah's face, when Del admitted that Noah was right.

Advertising the bar in local papers and via local businesses willing to partner with them was not enough. Establishing a social media presence for the bar was a must. And because Noah was scheduling meetings with the representatives from the Washington D.C. Major League Baseball team and the National Hockey League to become an approved venue for the teams and their fans in the Virginia area, he'd assigned social networking to Del since he was the manager of this growing establishment.

That thought had Del cursing and remembering to pull his phone from his back pocket. He activated the screen and saw that MercedesGirl926 had responded to his last message.

"You been on that phone a lot tonight," Ethan said. "Got a new lady in your life?"

"Mind yours," Del snarled and turned away.

Ethan chuckled and continued to fill the next drink order.

Del looked down at his phone again. A whisper of a smile flashed over his face. She didn't like roses and candlelight. He touched the screen to provide his response.

Del: I usually pass on them too.

Del picked up the live stream of the bar through something called a hashtag and had reluctantly joined in the conversation about the performance. MercedesGirl926 was running the video so Del presumed she was somewhere in the bar. There were dozens of women here tonight and truthfully, it wasn't as if he were looking for a personal connection. His goal was to simply interact so that Noah would get off his back about being a social mediaphobe. But MercedesGirl926 was chatting with everyone using witty comebacks and humorous observations. She'd also complimented the bar's hot wings and easy-going atmosphere. So, Del tried the private message button that lingered on the sidebar of the screen and a separate conversation had begun.

"That's what I'm talkin' about. This place has been packed since happy hour and the crowd doesn't seem to be dwindling down, even though it's getting late. Fellas, I'd say we're turning a corner," Noah announced as he joined them behind the bar.

"Yeah, and it would help immensely if both of you would stop standing around talking and actually help with this booming crowd," Ethan quipped.

The former Secret Service agent who was about to become the first of their close-knit group to take the plunge into matrimony, leaned over the bar to deliver two frilly looking drinks to two smiling women. Del stared at each of them, one with brilliant blue eyes and red hair that reminded him briefly of Jean Gray from the X-Men. The second one had beautiful caramel-hued skin and wore her hair in long golden strands.

Was one of them MercedesGirl926?

"Karaoke Night is a good idea," Noah continued. "With Sunday, Monday and Thursday nights reserved for football games and hosting all the Fantasy Leagues in the area, we're pretty set on crowds for those nights. NBA games on Tuesdays and Thursdays. College football on Saturdays. Wednesday and Fridays had a gap, but I'd say we've filled Friday surprisingly good."

Noah stood with his arms folded over his chest, nodding as he continued to look around the bar. Del couldn't help but agree with him, after he'd watched those two women walk away from the bar and return to the group they'd been standing with. A group that was evenly paired, men and women. A tall man with wire-framed glasses slipped his arm around the waist of the golden-loc woman, his fingers splaying over the curve of her ass as he pulled her tightly against his side. No way was she Mercedes-Girl926. This guy was barely letting her breathe, let alone releasing his grip on her long enough so that she could participate in a cyber-conversation for the last half hour.

"Don't forget Mrs. Tillman's warning that we do nothing to

conflict with the good people of Providence attending bible study and prayer service on Wednesday evenings," Ethan chimed in when he stopped moving around to stand beside them.

The three men stood together, just as they had throughout most of their lives. Also known as the town bad boys, they'd all had a rough time of it here in Providence. Nobody ever thought they'd amount to anything after those years they'd struggled to grow into men. But they'd each defied the odds by either heading off to college or the military and afterwards settling into good, respectable careers. It was just a strange twist of that evil and spiteful fate that had them all ending those wonderful careers within the same year and returning to the only home they knew. Now, fifteen months later, they were standing in the midst of their second chance at this thing called life. After pooling their money and the talents they'd each learned throughout the years, they'd opened Game Changers and were all hoping for its success.

"No problem there," Del said, with a nod of his head. "We're still in the praying business."

"You got that right," Noah added. "I'm gonna head over to the front. The crowd will start migrating to the doors in the next half hour as we head toward closing and I want to make sure there are no issues in the parking lots or on the streets."

"That's a good idea. I'll go over to the side entrance in a few minutes," Del said.

Noah was once an in-demand Hollywood stuntman, and while his broad frame had slimmed down quite a bit since his return to Providence and from the eighteen months he'd remained free of steroid use, he was still the best one of the group to hire and supervise the security team for the bar. The fact that this guy was also a marketing genius would come as a shock to many, but not Del. Noah had always been able to sell anything, starting with the individual mints they used to grab handfuls of from the therapists' office every boarder from Grace House was forced to see. The memory of how many sodas and snacks Noah had been able to buy them with the proceeds of selling those mints to the members of Pleasant Rose Baptist Church on the Sunday mornings they all marched into the building, was fresh and still funny in Del's mind.

"I'll text Rock to start shutting down upstairs," Ethan said before nudging Del. "Or would you rather do that since you've been on your phone half the night?"

"What? Del was on his phone while working? Somebody call the cops. He's broken his own staunch rule about paying attention to customers first and foremost," Noah added with a hearty chuckle.

Del didn't find either of them funny.

"Send your text and you get to the front door. I swear some kids never grow up," he said before pushing past Noah to move toward the end of the bar where he could step out onto the main floor.

"We're just following your example, as always, captain!" Noah yelled behind him.

Del didn't bother to turn back but flipped his middle finger to the duo as he left them standing there. They'd always called him captain, and not just because he'd managed to bring up his failing grades from eighth grade to his sophomore year in high school, enough that he could play on the football team. By his junior year, Del was on the honor roll and was named captain of the team. But, as the oldest of the six friends, he'd always been considered their leader. A title he'd never wanted but respected all the same.

He was just arriving at the side door when a large group were getting up from their seats to head out. He smiled and thanked them for coming, wishing them all a safe night as they proceeded through the door he held open. It was a brisk fall night, so he quickly pulled the door closed and stood to the side as he noted another table getting their jackets on as well. With his legs slightly parted, hands clenched in front of him, he smiled and nodded at their guests, feeling a humongous sense of pride at all that he and the brothers had managed to build here. That worked for Del's grand plan. He was determined that the small-minded people that still lived in this town were going to eat all the negative words they'd ever spouted about him and his friends, once and for all. They were running a fine, upstanding establishment that commanded respect.

The phone vibrating in his front pant pocket tugged Del's attention from his thoughts and he pulled it out expecting that either Rock or Ethan was texting him with a status of their crowd exiting for the night. He was wrong. Surprisingly so.

MercedesGirl926: Something else I like is a man with strong arms and a great mouth.

On Del's second turn reading the response, the word "mouth" had his dick jumping.

With a frown as his previous thoughts circled in his mind, Del wondered what the fine, upstanding citizens of Providence would think if they knew he was embroiled in a sexy conversation with a stranger he'd met online. His thumbs were moving as if they had a mind of their own, ignoring thoughts of anyone else but MercedesGirl926.

Del: I like a willing and hot mouth as well.

He typed the words and wished like hell he was going home to MercedesGirl926 lying in his bed, instead of stuffing the phone back into his pocket and forcing himself to smile, while his dick continued to throb.

2

*I*t was after two a.m. So why was she up, holding her phone in her hand, preparing to reply to yet another message from GCSports18?

Rylan was convinced she was losing her mind. These late-night conversations had been going every night for the last five days and in that time, she still hadn't asked what GCSports18's real name was. And he hadn't asked for hers. The subject just never came up, which seemed odd if she really thought about it.

Rylan: Owning your own business isn't easy, but it has its rewards.

She typed the response to his question about her day.

This is how the conversations always started. He asked about her day. She answered and then asked about his. He answered.

GCSports18: I'm sure it does. Today just wasn't one of them.

Rylan could totally relate to that. The body shop wasn't doing as much business as it normally did, even with winter weather making its first appearance by way of thirty-degree temperatures and the threat of their first snowstorm coming this weekend. This was usually the time people brought their vehicles in for everything from fluid checks to brake work, just to be prepared through the winter months. Breaking down on the side of the road in freezing temps or worse, a snowstorm, was not an ideal situation. But this year, it seemed, the majority of the car owners in Providence had vehicles in perfect condition.

On top of that, her father had officially moved out of the ranch style house on Broken Land Drive where Rylan grew up.

Today had actually been a pretty crappy day.

She didn't type that.

Rylan: Feeling kind of tired. Think I'll turn in.

She replied and then leaned over in her bed ready to put the phone on its charger and worry about all that was going on in her life until eventually falling asleep—her new nightly ritual.

The phone buzzed with a notification before she could put it down. She sighed, keeping the phone in hand before falling back against the pillows. She stared up to the ceiling but saw nothing because she'd already turned off the lights. The bedroom in her apartment was small. The apartment was small. A studio that seemed like a good idea when she'd leased it a year ago, since she lived alone, but lately had felt more like a box closing in on her. The wind that accompanied the chilly temps pressed against the single window in the bedroom causing a slight draft which required an extra fleece blanket on her bed.

GCSports18: If I were there I'd run you a hot bath. I'd fix hot chocolate and add lots of whipped cream. Just the way you like it.

She sighed while reading his words. She'd forgotten that she told him she preferred hot chocolate to wine. And it never dawned on her that he'd recall any of the things they'd talked about. This was just a casual chit-chat…that had turned into a nightly ritual.

Rylan: That sounds heavenly.

She replied truthfully.

Of course, she could've run her own bath when she'd come in

just after eight this evening. The makings of her favorite hot chocolate were stored in the cabinet next to the refrigerator in her postage-stamp sized kitchen. But she'd opted for a ten-minute shower and a glass of cranberry juice to go along with the grilled ham and cheese she'd fixed for dinner. That was her idea of a glamorous life.

GCSports18: Then I would rub you down from head to toe with warm oil, massaging all the tension and fatigue away.

Damn. Could she actually imagine the feel of his hands on her oiled body? Hell yeah, she could! And it was amazing. Rylan actually moaned as she closed her eyes and felt herself sinking deeper into the mattress with the thought. Her eyes opened a slit as she typed a response.

Rylan: And I would be forever in your debt.

His response was three smiley face emojis.

She grinned.

Rylan: What would you like as repayment?

GCSports18: A beer and a newspaper.

A giggle erupted and she slapped a hand over her mouth. Then she realized she was the only one in the room to hear it and pulled her hand away. His response was definitely not what she'd expected.

Rylan: That's what relaxes you?

GCSports18: Yup. But I wasn't finished. The beer and the paper bring me down from the day at work, but then the warmth of your mouth covering me immediately takes my attention away from the paper. And I look down to see your pretty face staring up at me.

Rylan froze. Well, she went totally still. She was already pretty chilly thanks to the drafty old windows in this place.

Rylan: You don't know how I look.

She cringed the minute she typed those words because she realized how silly they were considering the tone of this conversation. Surely her looks didn't matter in this fantasy they were developing. Not that she wasn't pretty, but it just didn't matter because they had never seen each other and had never discussed seeing each other.

GCSports18: We can change that. Let's meet.

Why in the hell had he typed that?

Del ran a hand down his face and shook his head. He was sitting in the black leather recliner across the room from his king-size bed. It was quiet. That was the reason he'd purchased this house at the far end of town, away from the business of Main Street and the traffic of the highway. Normally, that was what he loved most about this place. Tonight, not so much.

He didn't want to meet MercedesGirl926. His statement to her was ridiculous. Del wasn't looking for a woman. Despite his friends' crude jokes to the contrary, he was not in a perpetually bad mood because of his sexual drought. For one, not having sex in the last six months was a choice, not an affliction. His last affair had lasted exactly five dates, two of which ended at a hotel. After that, business had become the priority and there hadn't been time—or the inclination, he admitted only to himself—to search for companionship.

Yet every night for the last five days he'd come home from the bar, taken a shower, grabbed a beer and sat down in this chair with his phone in hand. The conversations with MercedesGirl926 had become the highlight of his evenings. But they were only words on a screen, nothing more.

He checked the phone. Ten minutes had passed and she hadn't responded. Del set the phone on the small table beside the recliner and stood. He took the few steps to the window and looked out to the tall trees just about hidden by the darkness. This was part of his nightly ritual too. If he thought about it too deeply, he'd admit that his personal life was as dark as the scenery. It hadn't always been that way, but Del was a big believer in karma, so he'd resigned himself to take his penance in whatever form it came.

The piercing buzz of his house alarm being set off yanked his attention from what couldn't be changed and Del immediately headed to the oak nightstand on the right side of his bed. He opened the bottom drawer and retrieved the Glock he kept there. In seconds he was across the room, his back against the wall, safety released on the gun held tightly in his right hand.

When the alarm continued to blare throughout the house, Del took the stairs, both arms held straight down in front of him as his hands gripped the gun. The moment his bare feet touched the floor in the front hallway, Del raised his arms and pointed the gun at the back of the person standing a few feet in front of him. Before he could make his standard, "turn around slowly with your hands up," command, a sense of familiarity hit him.

Lance spun around with his gun drawn.

"Remember we used to cops and robbers in the backyard," his twin brother said, a huge grin spreading across his face.

"I carry real bullets now," Del snapped and relaxed his stance before re-engaging the gun's safety mode. "Why the hell can't you remember the alarm code? I made it simple enough that you and Camy could never forget it."

He moved to the control panel beside the front door and punched in their mother's birthday.

"Forgot," Lance said from behind. "Got a lot on my mind tonight."

When the alarm was once again engaged, Del locked the door and turned to face his brother. He didn't bother asking Lance what was on his mind because he was certain he already knew. Their mother had loved the holiday season. The early years of their childhood were filled with huge Thanksgiving dinners with family coming from several east coast states to share with them and Christmas steeped in tradition and town festivities. After their father's untimely death from pneumonia when Del and Lance were eleven years and Camy was eight, their mother had worked even harder to keep the same celebratory feel to the season. Sometimes it worked. More times it didn't. Lance and Del both hated this time of year for similar, yet different reasons, but the common ground was their mother.

"Come on, let's get some coffee," Del said and headed for the kitchen.

"Don't want any," Lance replied. "I'm just going to accept the invitation to use your guest bedroom and pass out."

Lance was already on the stairs, one hand gripping the railing tightly as he attempted to navigate lifting one leg after another, the other hand still holding his gun. Del shook his head and went to his brother's side.

"You won't make it to the bed without hurting yourself or shooting a hole in my wall," Del told him as he relieved his brother of the gun.

"Hey, that's mine," Lance complained.

"I'll tuck it in bed beside you," Del told him.

He slid an arm around Lance's waist and felt his brother lean into him as they took the stairs together.

"You're a good guy, Del," Lance said, his words slightly slurred. "Fuck those DOJ idiots for everything they said about you. They don't know squat."

"Yeah," Del said even though the last thing he wanted to talk about tonight was the demise of his illustrious career as a DEA agent. "We'll get you into bed and I guess I'm taking your early shift at the bar tomorrow."

"The bar," Lance echoed as they walked into the bedroom across the hall from Del's. "Our bar."

"Yeah, it's ours," Del told him and despite the circumstances enjoyed the hell out of how that sounded.

He stood with his brother beside the bed and turned so that Lance could plop down onto the mattress. Del watched him immediately roll over onto his side, grabbing a pillow to tuck beneath his head. He was four minutes older than Lance. They were fraternal twins, but had similar body builds, the same sepia complexion, shared a love of all sports, and despised spinach and broccoli. They'd also both entered into law enforcement careers, only to have them come crashing down around them. His jaw clenched at the memory of the night he received the call that Lance had been shot. The sting of fear pierced his chest as if were just yesterday and not almost two years ago. Del couldn't take losing another person he loved and was grateful every day since, that his brother's life had been spared. Even if it meant Lance was sentenced to a form of living hell instead. The PTSD his twin suffered after the events of that fateful night was exacerbated by Lance's stubborn refusal to take the prescribed medication. Add to that the bitterness Lance still clung to after learning his girlfriend of eight years had left him for her trainer, and his brother was like a ticking time bomb. Del vowed to be there the moment he blew.

Del eased his hand behind his back, tucking Lance's gun in the waistband of his pants alongside his own. When he thought Lance was already asleep, Del removed his brother's shoes and turned to leave the room.

"You think she'd be proud of us?" Lance asked, his voice as soft as a child's.

Del stopped and hung his head low. They would both forever fight this same internal battle with guilt.

"I hope so," he replied.

Seconds later, he closed the door to the guest room and returned to his own where he sat once again in the recliner across from his bed. Del did hope that their mother would be proud of the way they'd begun to rebuild their lives yet again. He actually prayed daily that she would, but he wasn't certain. He knew he could never be certain because his mother was no longer here for them to ask.

On a heavy sigh, he picked up his phone. Still no response from MercedesGirl926. It was just as well. He was too tired to deal with any more conversation tonight. And he'd been through too much to think that meeting a woman online would help assuage the turmoil smoldering inside of him.

He got up from the chair and went to the nightstand to plug his phone into its charger. Then he climbed in his bed. He closed his eyes immediately and refused to let his mind wonder what MercedesGirl926 looked like, or how she kissed, or tasted. It didn't matter. Knowing wouldn't erase the past or change the future he knew he had to accept.

But it might ease the burning desire he'd developed for this woman whom he'd never seen. He could only hope.

3

"You're so tough and opinionated, why don't you buy it?"

Rylan hated a dare. And she definitely hated when it came from her older sister, Naomi.

"I've actually been considering that very option," Rylan replied and pressed the knife down so hard on the softened sweet potato that she almost chopped off her finger.

Her mother would have totally freaked if that happened. Not because Rylan would have been fingerless and probably bleeding profusely, but because said blood would be splattered all over Estelle's newly renovated, pristine kitchen.

"You are not buying that rundown body shop," Estelle chimed in. "That's just ridiculous and a total waste of your life. It's bad enough you've spent the bulk of your formative years under the hood of a car wearing grease smudges instead of MAC products. But I will not stand by and watch you throw away your future to such a dingy and worthless effort."

The judgmental and chastising tone was Estelle Janet Kent's trademark. The former ballet dancer turned math teacher and in the last five years principal of Old Kenton Middle School, Estelle was the epitome of Black elegance. From the stylish clothes that flanked her still-svelte at fifty-eight figure, to her impeccably styled ink black hair and expertly applied make-up, she was educated, classy and not-to-be-messed with. Especially not by her youngest and most disappointing child.

Rylan retrieved the chunk of potato that had rolled across the marble-top counter, dropping it into the bowl in front of her.

"It's our legacy," Rylan said in a tone lower and more subdued than she was accustomed to using. Except for whenever she was around her mother and Naomi. They were a dynamic duo that Rylan had never quite adjusted to, even after being around them for all of her twenty-seven years of life.

"My legacy is not dirt and grime," Naomi said. And as if her words hadn't made her point clear enough, the way her sister crinkled her perfectly pert nose and rolled her pretty brown eyes, reflected every bit of the disgust she felt toward Kent Automotive.

"Fifteen pageant titles, domestic and international. Interviews in Marie Clare and Vogue. A degree in political science and dating Ellis Colby, star NBA point guard, is a legacy," Naomi announced with a wink in Rylan's direction.

Rylan shook her head and returned her attention to the sweet potatoes. Naomi was thirty-two years old. She was five feet, ten inches tall with amber-colored eyes and a tawny complexion. Her hair was in a messy but chic style today, dark brown with honey gold highlights. She wore a lacy top that tied in the back and hunter green slacks. The most casual thing she'd done since walking through the door of their parents' house was take off the five-inch heeled natural-colored pumps and walk barefoot into the kitchen.

Naomi was everything Rylan wasn't.

"Look, you have your interests and I have mine," Rylan added. "It's always been that way and that's fine. I've worked with

Dad at the auto shop since I was seven years old. It's what I love to do."

"You would've found something else to love if you'd gone away to college like I wanted you to. You were accepted into Spellman, UC Berkley, Howard, and Georgetown. And those were just the places I applied to for you. If you'd put your mind to it you could've gone anywhere and become anything," Estelle told her while reaching into a cabinet and taking out a glass bowl for the white potatoes she was peeling for potato salad.

"I like working on cars," Rylan said in defense. "That's why I went to trade school instead of college. I wanted to perfect all the skills Dad had already taught me. And since then I've taken business and accounting classes at the community college. I can run Kent Automotive in every aspect now."

"And because of your father's gambling and drinking, you've been doing exactly that for the last couple of years. But no more, I can promise you that, Rylan. This nonsense stops here and now," Estelle said adamantly. "We're selling the auto shop so that your father can reimburse me for the shares of his retirement fund that he gambled away trying to save that damn place."

Rylan set the knife down because now her hands were shaking. She picked up the bowl of butter and put it into the microwave to melt. This wasn't the conversation she'd wanted to have today. She'd come to the house where she'd grown up, that her mother now lived in alone, at ten in the morning to start helping with preparations for tomorrow's Thanksgiving dinner. She didn't come here to argue.

"Dad's been going through a lot in the past few years. I'm only stating a fact, not making excuses for him," Rylan added because she knew what her mother was going to say even before she said it.

"The shop was losing money and he did what he thought he could to save it. Gambling wasn't the right move. I've told him that. But I'm going to find a way to make this work, because it's my livelihood now, Mama. It's my life that you're so vehemently talking about selling off," she said.

"Get a new life," Estelle snapped. "If you can admit that your father and his ridiculous, lazy way of thinking was wrong, then you can walk away. It's as simple as that. You can still get into Berkley and go for a master's in business since you're interested in running things."

"I'm interested in running the auto shop," Rylan insisted.

"She's interested in being Greasy Peasy all her life," Naomi interjected. "Don't even waste your time trying to talk sense into her, Mama. You know how stubborn she is."

And that was Naomi's not-so-gentle slap-in-the-face way of helping Rylan out of the conversation she'd had with her mother all of her life. The only good decisions Rylan could ever make were the ones orchestrated by Estelle. Any of her own thoughts were wrong on one level or another because Rylan wasn't the second daughter that Estelle had wanted.

"It's a waste of time, Rylan. You're a pretty and smart girl. You can do anything you want with your life," Estelle continued.

Rylan whirled around to face her mother. "I am doing what I want with my life!"

Silence immediately fell over the room. Rylan and her mother stared at each other. Naomi picked up her phone and stared at it. And the microwave dinged.

"Ellis is coming for dinner tomorrow!" Naomi screamed. "He'll be here in the morning. We have to get this place cleaned up. And Rylan, don't mess up the sweet potato pie because that's Ellis's favorite."

Rylan didn't want to hear another word about Ellis—even though he'd scored an amazing 47 points in the playoffs last year —so she opened the microwave door and removed the bowl of melted butter.

"Don't worry about my pies, Naomi. I've got this. That's why you're only allowed to chop the food and not actually cook anything," she quipped.

Naomi rolled her eyes but didn't bother to reply because she knew Rylan was right.

The conversation in the Kent kitchen immediately shifted to Ellis Colby and how much he was worth, to a possible summer wedding even though there hadn't been an official proposal. Rylan kept quiet and continued working. She had nothing to add to the discussion of wedding colors, event planners or honeymoon locations. She'd never thought about who she would marry or what their wedding would look like. Probably because in all her years of dating she'd deduced that relationships were overrated and sexual pleasure could be a solo achievement.

Rylan also didn't believe in the butterflies dancing in the stomach which Naomi was now describing about each time she was with Ellis. Rylan had never experienced that when with any of her dates. Eager anticipation was what her mother called it, followed by more flowery and romantic words. Rylan kept mashing the sweet potatoes, butter, brown sugar and cinnamon. She'd never anticipated any date with a guy. She had, however, looked forward to her nightly chats with GCSports18, which was all the way ridiculous because she had no idea who he was.

But she could find out. Last night he'd said they should meet. Today, Rylan wondered if he was right.

Del frowned at his phone for the billionth time today. He stuffed it into his pocket at the exact moment that Camy walked into the living room.

"You on your phone again?" she asked as she passed where he sat on the couch and dropped down on the other end. "The bar's closed for the holiday so nobody's texting you about an emergency down there. "

Del knew the bar was closed. He'd been there at quarter to nine when they'd wished the last customers of the night a happy Thanksgiving. The guys unanimously agreed to close early tonight and remain closed until noon on Friday. Even though they'd each had a rough start in life, they all recognized the importance of family and spending holidays with them instead of at a bar drinking. Which was why he'd come to his childhood home where his sister now lived alone, to offer his help with the family dinner she was hosting tomorrow. Of course, he'd come once all the preparations were completed, but he'd decided to stay and keep Camy company for a while anyway. He wouldn't tell her that he was actually the one who needed the company.

"I know," he replied. "The bar's all locked up for the night."

"You guys are doing good there," Camy said as she reached for the remote control.

Del let her take it. He wasn't watching whatever was playing on the television anyway.

"Hosting the kids' football league barbeque last weekend was a fabulous idea," she continued as she changed channels. "It was so much fun watching them all run around the park, eat and have fun."

Del nodded. "Yeah. That was Ethan's idea. He and Portia have lots of plans for activities for the young people in Providence and once Game Changers Safe House opens, we'll all be chipping in to offer unique programs to carry out throughout the year."

"That's what's up," Camy said and leaned over to slap him on the shoulder. "You guys have been doing a lot of good in the community since you've been back."

"Not enough for some people," Del snapped.

Camy shook her head, knowing who he was talking about without him having to recount the run-in he'd had with his arch-nemesis yesterday. "He's an ass. He was jealous of you in high school when you made captain of the football team and took all the girls, and he was even more jealous when you got into the DEA at such a young age. No matter what you do, Mal Penning is always going to dislike you. But that's his problem, not yours."

Del and Mal had a history. It was a dark and sometimes dangerous history stemming from the time Del broke Mal's nose when they were sixteen and culminating with part of the reason Del resigned from the DEA. The fact that Mal was now in a position of authority over him wasn't sitting well with Del. But as always, he was trying to handle the situation as diplomatically as possible.

He leaned forward resting his elbows on his knees. "You sound just like her."

Camy chuckled. "I'm her daughter. And you're her son. She raised us to be confident and compassionate and to look out for each other. Which is why I've been going to the town council meetings and speaking up each time Mal tries to slide in something negative about you and the guys. Others in Providence see what he's trying to do and they're on your side too."

"I don't want anybody choosing sides. I want them to accept that people can change. We all changed," he said.

"You got that right," she quipped. "I've never seen you checking your phone as much as I have in the past few days. You texting someone special?"

Del shook his head and smiled. His sister was tenacious and nosy as hell.

"Nobody special," he told her, even though he wondered what MercedesGirl926 really was to him. And why he couldn't go one day without thinking about her.

"But you are texting someone?" she continued.

Del shook his head. "No. I wasn't texting anyone."

Camy narrowed her eyes at him. "Was someone texting you?"

"No," he replied.

She sighed heavily. "Would you tell me if they were?"

He shook his head once more. "No."

She pushed him again. "You always were the secretive one."

Del laughed. The first time he'd done so all day. "And you were always the dreamy one. Please change this channel because I do not want to watch these silly holiday movies about the couple that falls in love two hours after they swore they were against falling in love."

Camy laughed and tucked the remote under the pillow she was leaning against. "Well that's just too bad because my television stays on this channel from late October until after New Year's Day. Love and holiday festivities are definitely in the air!"

Del groaned and was about to say something about regretting coming over here when the sound of the ringing doorbell interrupted them.

"When I come back, I want to see something else on this television," he said, getting up to answer the door.

"There's nothing else on."

"Sure, there is," he yelled over his shoulder. "*Die Hard* is a Christmas movie, see if that's on."

"That is not a Christmas movie and I'd much rather watch a couple fall in love than Bruce Willis tossing some guy off a building," Camy replied.

Del was about to reply that was the best part of the movie when he entered the small foyer and opened the door.

"Hey Del," Rylan said before walking past him and into the house.

"Hey Rylan," he spoke and closed the door.

It was getting late and while Del knew that Rylan and Camy had been best friends forever, he wondered why she was out alone at this time of night. Then he shook his head as he walked back into the living room.

"Hey, you're just in time for the next movie," Camy was saying to Rylan by the time Del entered the living room again.

"Oh no, girl are you still watching these silly romances," Rylan quipped.

"Thank you!" Del said with more enthusiasm than was probably necessary. "I was just trying to tell her there had to be something else on television that we could watch."

Rylan nodded. "Seriously, Camy, there has to be something else."

"Why is everyone so against holidays and love? You two need to find your happy ever after, or a drink or something," Camy said.

Del watched his sister stand and had the good sense to duck as she tossed one of the decorative pillows off the couch in his direction.

"I'm getting a drink," she announced. "Anybody else want something?"

"Cranberry juice," Rylan yelled.

"Beer," Del said.

He sat on the loveseat across from the couch and looked over to ask Rylan how she was doing, but snapped his lips shut when he saw her leaning over. Actually, what he saw was the curve of her ass in jeans that looked as if they were made specifically for her. He closed his eyes immediately because, what the fuck?

Rylan was his sister's friend. Hell, she was damn near a sister to him. How many times had Rylan spent the night at their house, been at the table first thing in the morning eating cereal right alongside him and Lance? Wherever Camy was, Rylan wasn't far behind. Except when Camy sang, danced or was on the cheerleading squad, Rylan was usually at her dad's body shop. When the hell did the tomboy get a woman's body?

"It's about time," she said and Del's eyes shot open.

"What?"

Rylan was sitting on the couch now, the remote in hand as she held it up in triumph.

"I found the remote," she announced with a smile and immediately changed the channel.

A really nice smile, Del thought.

Her hair came to her chin, black with golden highlights, in what looked like soft waves. She removed her leather jacket. The yellow t-shirt she wore was as tight as her jeans, the material smoothly stretching over palm-size breasts. She kicked off the short black boots she was wearing before tucking her legs beneath her.

"There," she said when he was too dumfounded to speak another word. "*Christmas Vacation*. That's a holiday movie worth watching."

"Absolutely," he replied, rubbing a hand down his face and taking a deep breath.

He was trippin'. Rylan wasn't sexy. The woman he was really thinking about was MercedesGril926. It was her body that Del wanted to see. Her long legs he wanted wrapped around his waist as he plunged deep into her. Not Rylan, who he knew hated ketchup and couldn't dance to save her life but could ride a bike and hold a wheelie for longer than any of the guys that had lived on their block.

"Wait. Who changed the channel?" Camy asked when she came back into the room.

"Not me," Rylan answered quickly and tossed the remote across the room to Del.

He caught it without a second's thought and tucked it under the pillow of the loveseat.

"Oh, so that's the game we're playing now," Camy said with a frown as she put the glasses on the table and tossed the beer to Del. "Well, I don't really care. It's a Christmas movie so I'm good."

Camy plopped down on the couch beside Rylan and crossed her legs. "I love the holidays."

Rylan looked at Del. He shrugged and they both grinned. His sister was something. And Rylan, well, she was his sister's best friend.

The movie was halfway over when Del thought he felt his phone vibrate. He dug into his pocket and pulled it out, only to sigh with disappointment at the sight of a text message from Lance letting Del know that he would not be crashing at his place tonight. That meant his brother had probably found a woman to spend the evening with instead. Del sighed as he stared at the television once more. He wished he were spending the evening differently. Perhaps with MercedesGirl926 was a thought.

4

*D*el: Been thinking about you all night.

It was easy to admit that via messages.

MercedesGirl926: I thought about you too.

That made him feel good.

Tonight had been mad busy at the bar with people coming in after concluding their Black Friday shopping at the outlet mall just down the road. All hands had been on deck with the guys pulling double duties and shifts and calling in mostly all of their staff to do the same. Business had definitely been good, but damn he was tired as hell and feeling edgier than he had in he couldn't even remember when.

After a quick, hot shower when he came home, Del passed on the beer and grabbed a bottle of water instead. On the ride home, he'd thought about the other half of a foot-long hoagie he had left over in the fridge, but now, he'd decided against that as well. What he really wanted wasn't going to be found in his refrigerator. He wanted to talk to MercedesGirl926 more than he wanted to eat.

Their messaging had resumed hours after he'd finished watching movies with Camy and Rylan, with both of them ignoring his request to meet. They'd simply continued chatting as if that comment hadn't been made. She wasn't looking forward to Thanksgiving any more than he had been. Even though they didn't discuss the specifics of why, they were still able to commiserate together. She did mention being stressed about her business and Del had wondered what kind of work she did. Instead of asking, he offered some advice based on his newfound experience and the business classes he'd taken last year. She'd been very receptive and thanked him as if he'd answered some sort of prayer when all he'd done was convey some of the organizational tips he'd learned and a bit of the marketing stuff Noah had taught him. Still, it had made Del feel good to read the lighter, more relieved tone of her messages.

In return, chatting with her had lifted some of the stress Del had been feeling as he contemplated what he was going to do about the subpoena he'd received to testify in the final drug bust of his law enforcement career. There was also the issue of Lance and how he was coping with his life's changes. Del didn't want to admit that thinking about either of those things struck a chord of fear in him. So instead, he reluctantly accepted that his friends may have been right all along. These burdens Del was carrying might not be as heavy if he'd found some sort of relief.

Preferably of the sexual kind.

Del: Never thought this much about a woman before.

He was sitting in his recliner, the towel still wrapped around his waist. It was dark in his room at almost four in the morning.

MercedesGirl926: It would be cliché if I said the same to you, but since I'm up at this insane hour waiting for our nightly chat, I guess my actions speak for me.

Del's grin was slow, but wide as it spread while he read those words. Why did this woman make him feel so good, when all the others had failed?

Del: I would hope we could be honest and real. No pretenses or misconceptions.

He typed that as he thought about his previous personal relationships. Del never had problems getting girls in high school, or college for that matter. And he enjoyed every minute of their fun-filled, carefree, sexual relations. But there'd never been anything more. He'd been chatting with MercedesGirl926 for three weeks now and felt closer to this woman he'd never met in person, than he had all the women he'd lay in bed with naked.

MercedesGirl926: That's the only way I know how to be.

Del let his head fall back against the leather recliner. He closed his eyes and took a deep breath, releasing it slowly as what he wanted to say to her next played through his mind. He'd thought about it all night at the bar. What he wanted from her? What he thought he could handle? What might be disrespectful to her, or to him? All of the questions and answers had run in circles until this very moment.

Del: I'd like to see you.

He hit send but immediately followed that message with another.

Del: Send me a picture of any part of you. Just something so that I know this is real.

He stared at the words on his phone's screen and considered how insane this woman probably thought he was. His heart beat wildly in his chest while he waited for her response.

It didn't come quickly and he wondered if, once again, he'd said the wrong thing. She'd said she only knew how to be honest. Well, he was being honest. He couldn't stop thinking about her, and in a very sexual way. How that was possible if he'd never seen her before, Del couldn't say. And yes, this physical urgency was his fault. If he hadn't gone so long without, maybe he wouldn't be as needy as he'd been feeling in the past week. The other part however, she'd contributed to equally. If she weren't so easy to talk to, so down to earth and interesting, then he wouldn't be as drawn to her as he was. He wouldn't have wanted to send that first private message to her and he certainly wouldn't have kept the insane hours he did just so that he could communicate with her.

The phone buzzed and Del hurriedly looked at the screen.

MercedesGirl926: Not over this site. What's your number?

They were on a social network site. Sometimes Del forgot about that as they messaged back and forth. He'd detested social media so much in the years since it had blossomed that he couldn't believe he'd actually been using it as much as he had in the past month. Of course, that was work related and this wasn't.

She wanted his number so she could text him a picture. He closed his eyes and sighed. This was such a bad idea. How many phone lines had he dumped during the course of an investigation? Thousands. And how many of those phone dumps also consisted of text messages, photos and any other history stored on cell phones? Again, thousands. And each time he'd shaken his head at how much information people voluntarily gave away via electronic devices. Didn't they know that nothing was safe from those who either had the power, or ones who had the inclination to find it?

Maybe they did and just didn't care.

He must be in that category, because Del typed in his number.

A couple minutes later his phone buzzed again.

Del saved the number to his contacts under her screen name. Then he went back to the text and looked at the picture.

His body tightened, dick stretching until the towel was tented.

The picture was of one long, bare leg. Skin almost the exact deep brown color as his on a perfectly formed calf and thigh that looked soft to the touch. His finger hoovered at the very edge of the phone's screen as Del wondered if he swiped left, would he be treated to what was beyond that lovely thigh.

Now, he was aroused and flummoxed as he considered sending her a picture in return. It was only fair to put himself out there in the same way he'd requested of her. It took a few tries because in addition to hating social media, he was only in the habit of using his phone to check email and text messages and make calls. When he finally had an agreeable shot, he sent the picture of his bare chest and waited like he'd just turned in a test for grading.

Her response eventually appeared.

MercedesGirl926: Can I amend my answer to a question you asked a while ago?

He didn't know what to say and it didn't matter because she sent another text.

MercedesGirl926: When you asked what I liked. I didn't have this pic. I definitely like a well-defined chest.

He grinned like a kid.

Del: And I definitely like long legs that can be wrapped tightly around my waist.

MercedesGirl926: There was a time when I was called gangly. But now my long limbs could wrap around your waist and your neck securing me tightly against you.

He swallowed and let his legs fall open. His dick was so hard it ached and he finally unhooked the towel so that it slipped down into the chair and his bobbing erection was free.

Del: I'd like you wrapped around me. I'd like to be deep inside you.

MercedesGirl926: So deep I would feel completely full. I'd like that very much.

Del: How much? Enough that you would use your fingers to act as if I were actually there with you right now?

In the time that Del waited for a response, he used a hand to grab his erection, wrapping his fingers tightly around its base and squeezing.

MercedesGirl926: We do it at the same time. Five seconds after you read this message, put your phone down and act as if I were there.

He groaned after reading those words. Was he really doing this? He was a thirty-one-year-old man who was more than capable of finding a date and having a woman in his bed at any moment. He didn't have to resort to sexting or online dating of any sort. Yet, here he was, wanting desperately to do anything she said.

He placed the phone on the table beside the recliner and lay his head back against the cool leather. She'd said he should act as if she were there with him. What would he do if she were? What would he want her to do?

Del wanted her legs wrapped around him, just as he'd said. Still able to see the picture she'd sent clearly in his mind, he closed his eyes and imagined both long, dark brown legs rubbing against his waist. Her skin would be smooth, legs strong as she lifted her hips and adjusted herself so the bare flesh of her center could ease down over him. His hand began to move over his length. Up and down in a series of quick motions. He imagined her wherever she lived, lying on her bed, legs spread, fingers working her hot pussy, the way he was working his dick.

If he were there with her, he'd put his mouth where her fingers undoubtedly were now. He'd suck the plump folds of her pussy, press his tongue against the tight bud of her clit. Del's hand moved slower for a moment as he circled his wrist, up and then back down again. His breathing quickened until he could hear himself panting loudly.

In his mind she was moving her hips now, lifting them slightly off the bed. Two fingers would ease into her moist opening while the other pressed against her clit. She would arch her back and moan. Del's ministrations grew faster. He pumped mercilessly into his hand. Her fingers would move faster, sliding in and out as her essence dripped slowly. She was panting now. He could hear her sweet, sex-husky voice echoing in his head. His mouth was open as his panting turned to all out moans, his hand moving faster while the other gripped the arm of the recliner. He lifted his hips, pumping fiercely while swirling his wrist, his hand creating a magnificent friction up and down his rigid length. She would scream with her release. Del grunted and moaned as his spurted and oozed down his hand. He thrust his hips in a stiff motion, still pumping his length until his heart beat as if it might thump right out of his chest.

When his breathing had almost returned to normal, Del stood. He walked into the bathroom and cleaned himself before returning to his bedroom and pulling on a pair of shorts. He removed the towel from the recliner and tossed it into the hamper before picking up his phone from the table. There was no new text or message from MercedesGirl926.

Del moved toward his bed. He plugged the phone into the charger and sat down heavily.

Was he making a complete fool of himself for a woman he might never see?

You were wonderful last night.

Rylan read the text for the hundredth time today while sitting in her car. She'd just pulled into the parking lot and cut the engine when she took her phone off the car charger and was about to slip it into the back pocket of her jeans. She was heading into Game Changers for a much-needed drink. To say it had been a rough day at the shop would be an under-statement.

Yet each time she'd read the message GCSports18 had sent a little after ten this morning, she somehow felt better. Just like last night, or rather even earlier this morning as she'd lay in her bed waiting for his nightly messages as if she were some love-struck teenager. Who was she kidding? Rylan hadn't experienced a soul-shattering crush, or any form of unrequited love as a teenager, because she hadn't dated until Ty Givens, one of the students in her trade school class. Just as puberty had seemed to skip right over her, so had experience with boys. Still, Rylan witnessed her fair share of tears and hopelessness by way of Camy who fell in and out of love with the speed of light. Her best friend had always been prettier and shapelier than Rylan. Just as Naomi was, but Rylan refused to keep count of the bad breaks she was dealt in life.

Why did GCSports18 only contact her in the middle of the night?

That thought sprang to mind as Rylan slipped the phone into her back pocket and pressed the button on her keychain to engage the alarm system on her car. The 1969 Mercedes 280SL Roadster was Rylan's sixteenth birthday present from her father, and thus her most cherished possession. She crossed the street and reached for the front door of the bar but paused before pulling it open because another thought occurred to her. A thought that made her feel sick to her stomach and angry as hell.

What if GCSports18 was married? Was that why he only messaged her at night? When his wife and perhaps his kids were in bed asleep while he sat in his den having phone sex with her?

Her cheeks warmed and she yanked the door open. The noise from a full house at the bar greeted her. Music sounded in the background while on the wall of televisions directly across from the bar college football games, MSNBC, a music video channel, and a documentary on Serena Williams played. She waved at Maxie who was at the hostess stand using the tablet to find seating for the next person in the short waiting line and kept moving until she was on the red plush carpeted stairs that led up to the Skybox. The rope that usually blocked the space and signaled a private event was in progress on the upper level was down, so she was allowed to go up to the quieter area in the bar.

Rylan needed to unwind. She was being stiffed for a four-thousand-dollar bill and holding the 2016 Lamborghini Aventador hostage wasn't as effective as she'd planned. She needed that money and about twenty-one thousand more in order to make the down payment and get the small business loan from the bank.

"Hey Slick!"

Rylan looked toward the bar where Rock was standing and lifted a hand to wave at him. She'd thought about dropping down into one of the red leather couches and ordering a steady flow of vodka shots until she passed out, but sitting at the bar gazing at the six foot four Samoan former pro wrestler definitely had its own decompressing benefits.

"Hey. Quiet up here tonight," Rylan said while sliding onto a bar stool.

Rock wore jeans and a fitted gray t-shirt with the Game Changers name and logo on the left side. His inky black hair was pulled back and most likely bound by a black ban as usual. Rylan never considered herself a fan of long hair on men, but Rock definitely pulled it off well.

"Yeah. I opened up here as overflow for downstairs. But only the regulars know to come on up," he said. "What can I get you?"

"Vodka," she replied and held up a finger.

Rock raised one thick eyebrow in question.

She rolled her eyes. "Alright, put it in a glass with ice to water it down, Dad," she snapped, exaggerating the last word.

Rock's family lived down the street from her while they were growing up. He had two older sisters that Naomi hung out with, but Rock felt as if he were a big brother to all four of them. At that time, he'd been a pain in the ass, but Rylan had missed him terribly in the years he'd been away at college and then traveling on the wrestling circuit.

He smiled and gave her a nod. "Good girl."

"I am over the legal drinking age, you know," she countered.

"And you're also driving back to your apartment alone. So, one vodka on the rocks coming up," he said.

Rylan looked away from him in mock disdain. She lifted her arms over her head, clasping her fingers together as she stretched and tried to let thoughts of the body shop and the marital status of the mysterious GCSports18 slip from her mind. Her phone buzzed as she brought her arms back down to her side and she grabbed it from her back pocket. She ignored the text message from her mother and set the phone on the bar top. Rock delivered her drink. Rylan didn't waste a second but picked up the glass and emptied it in two gulps.

"Another one," she said and tapped on the bar to get Rock's attention.

When he gave her a knowing look, Rylan reminded him that she was a paying customer, before getting up to go to the restroom. She, at least knew, how to pay for services that were rendered, or in this case, alcoholic beverages, as a normal person would. Why hadn't the rich guy from D.C. who dropped his car off at her shop two weeks ago learned that basic lesson in life? Damn, she was in a horrible mood. Which was shocking because this morning she'd awakened with her body still humming from the intense orgasm she'd had only hours before. The orgasm that had been precipitated by a gorgeously sculpted chest pic and the messages of a man she'd never seen before.

Rylan once again sat at the bar. She sipped slowly on her second drink because she knew Rock was going to protest heavily about giving her another one. As her mind would not be quieted and she felt she had to choose the lesser of two evils, she picked up her phone and started to send him a text. If he was married, it would serve him right if his wife picked up his phone at some point and learned of his wandering ways. Great, she sounded just like her mother when Estelle had first assumed Will was staying out so late at night because he was with another woman. Of course, it turned out her father had only cheated on his wife and family with the casino that had left him practically broke. Rylan opened the app instead and sent him a message.

Rylan: How was your day?

That's how he always started their conversations. Tonight, she would be the initiator. She checked the time and noted it was just after eight. Was he at home right now, having dinner with his wife two daughters and two sons? Was his minivan parked in the driveway as his family prepared to watch *A Christmas Story* or some other holiday movie? She took another drink to help wash away the thoughts that were now giving her a headache.

Why should she even care? They were just chatting. Right? Okay, this morning was more than a chat, but really, it wasn't that big of a deal. Rylan had masturbated before. So many times. And he was a grown man, she was fairly certain he'd gotten himself off more than once in his lifetime. So, there, no big deal. Except she'd thought about that not-a-big-deal episode most of the day. It had been the first time she'd been able to vividly imagine that the fingers on her heated flesh actually belonged to a man, instead of herself. And oh, had it felt so good. She closed her eyes to the thought and then startled when she heard the low moan.

Dammit! Was that her?

Her eyes shot open and she sat up straighter on the stool. She needed another drink. Shaking her head with that thought, she was just setting her glass down again when her phone buzzed.

GCSports18: Pretty good. Just about to get off work for the night.

Oh wow! He'd replied. And it wasn't after midnight. What did that mean?

Rylan: I just got off too. Are you busy tonight? Do you want to get a drink?

Her thumbs were moving faster than her brain and before she could stop herself, she hit send.

What the hell was she doing?

Did she want to see him? And when she did see him, what was going to happen next? Sex with a stranger? That was a whole different ball game compared to phone sex in the privacy of her own bedroom.

GCSports18: Sure. But I'm hungry. Let's meet at Margie's. 9:00?

So, he did live in Providence. She'd been fairly certain of that fact since they'd both been here at the bar the night they'd first met. But now he wanted to meet at Margie's in forty-five minutes. She dropped her phone back onto the bar top as if it had burned her fingers.

"Angry with your phone?" Rock asked as he walked by and caught the phone before it could topple over the edge of the bar onto his carefully stacked glasses.

Rylan shook her head and shrugged. "No. Ah, it just fell out of my hand."

"Uh huh. Well, I'll get you a glass of water," he said and held the phone out to her.

But before Rylan could grab the phone, it vibrated. The screen lit up and Rock looked down at it.

"Oh, you're on that app too?" he asked. "Noah said it was really popular. That's why he wanted the bar to have a page so we could advertise all our events and things like that."

"Really?" Rylan asked as she tried not to snatch the phone out of his hand. Instead she accepted it in as normal a way as possible. The last thing she needed was for Rock to see her receiving messages about having a hook-up tonight.

Was that what it was going to be? A hook-up? If so, she needed to run home and grab a really quick shower. She was grimy from being at the body shop all day and didn't have on the correct underwear.

"What's the page name so I can follow you?" she asked, trying to keep their conversation casual, even though her mind was whirling with thoughts of her online booty call.

"I think it's just the name of the bar. But you should really ask Del since he manages the page and does all the posting and stuff. His screen name is GCSports18 because he was incapable of coming up with anything more original," Rock told her.

Rylan had already begun typing in the screen name without really listening to what Rock had said. But when she did, she paused. Her heart suddenly skidded to an almost halt in her chest. The periodic thump was loud and the pit of dread forming in her stomach was hot.

"Did you say this was Del's screen name? As in Delano Greer, the serious and stoic one of the brothers?" Rylan asked.

"Yeah," Rock said and laughed. "He hates social media, but Noah insisted that as the manager Del get online and start helping to bring in customers. And you know what's funny? The past few weeks we've been seeing him with the phone in his hand a lot. And customers have been pouring in all the way from D.C. for the special events he's been posting."

Rylan couldn't continue typing the screen name. Her fingers were shaking.

"Del is GCSports18," she whispered.

Of course, he was, *Game Changers Sports* Bar and Del's number on his football jersey in high school was *18*.

It was a joke. It had to be. A very cruel and horrifying one.

Every message, from the very first one had to be a joke. Del and Lance used to play them on her and Camy all the time when they were younger. Rylan could recall numerous occasions when she'd slept over at Camy's and the guys had done things like put a box of frogs in Camy's closet so when they opened it, the frogs all jumped out scaring them half to death. Or the time when the twins had actually dared the then eight-year-old girls to watch *Scream* alone and then dressed in that dreadful costume for Halloween to continue scaring the crap out of them. It had been an ongoing and hilarious effort on the twins' part to torture Camy and Rylan, until Mr. Greer passed away and Mrs. Greer began crying instead of inviting Rylan over and setting up cute little tea parties for her and Camy.

Dammit!

What if Del really was playing a joke on her now? What if he knew exactly who she was all along and just continued this little prank for…for what? What would he get out of it now, except for some dirty conversation and a picture of her bare leg? An orgasm. That's what Rylan had gotten out of it? But what about Del? Had he been jerking off while she'd been playing with herself this morning?

Her face felt flushed and she couldn't stop her hands from shaking.

"I gotta go," she mumbled and then turned to slip off the stool.

"You okay?" Rock called behind her. "I can step out for a few and drive you home."

Rylan shook her head hard enough to exacerbate the headache she'd been nursing.

"I'm fine," she lied and headed for the steps.

She was anything but fine. She was mortified and pissed off.

And she couldn't wait to get out of this bar and to get home where she could…what? What was she going to do when she went home? Yell? Scream? Hate herself for falling for another one of the Greer Twins' stupid stunts?

Rylan had no idea. She just needed to get out of there. She walked fast, not really seeing anyone and pushing past the people who did end up in her path. When she pushed against a particularly hard chest and felt the slight grip of hands on her shoulders in response, she snapped out of the red haze of fury in time to look up into Del's dark brown eyes.

"Hey, kiddo. You okay?" he asked.

Was that concern in his tone or laughter in his eyes?

Rylan yanked out of his grasp. "I'm fine!" she shouted for what seemed like the billionth time and circled around him to get to the door.

The cool air immediately smacked her in the face as she pushed through the doors and started toward the spot where she'd parked her car.

"Rylan!"

He was right behind her. Shouting her name as if she didn't know it. But she knew her name and she knew his…GCSports18.

Del caught up to her just as she put her hand on the car door handle.

"Hey. Did something happen in there? Talk to me," Del said and something shifted in her chest.

No. He wasn't concerned about her. It was all a joke.

She took a deep, steadying breath and then found the courage to look him in the eye. But even that was different. She'd known Del forever and had thought he was a good-looking guy. That was it. Now, staring up at him after learning that he was the one she'd been waiting up every night to chat with, she saw someone totally different. His jaw seemed stronger. The dark hair of his lightly trimmed beard and mustache appeared more pronounced, giving him an edgy and sexy appeal. Even his eyes were darker, masked with desire. Oh no, she sounded just like Camy, being fanciful.

Correction, she was being an idiot!

"It's nothing. Work stuff," she mumbled and shifted from one foot to the other.

He nodded but didn't look as if he totally believed her.

"Yeah, your dad was in a couple nights ago and he talked a bit about the body shop. I'm sorry things aren't going too well," he said.

"Really? You're sorry. Because I seem to recall you frowning and judging me each time you brought your old clunker into the shop and realized I would be the one working on it," she snapped and hated how petty she sounded for bringing up something so far in the past.

Del had upgraded substantially since driving that old Chevy Impala. These days he rode through town in a shiny smoke gray Escalade with Greer18 on the tags.

Damn, she should've known GCSports18 was him.

"You know what, don't answer that. You don't have to say anything else. I'm okay, really. I just need to get home and sleep this mad off," she told him.

He nodded slowly. "Sure. But if somebody inside pissed you off. If anybody said something to irritate you, Rylan, you can tell me. I'll take care of it."

A bit of the steam she'd worked up sifted away at those words. As much of a tomboy as Rylan knew she'd been growing up, there'd never been a shortage of big brothers in town who were all willing to stand up for her. It was one of the things that had kept her from feeling so low whenever Naomi won a beauty pageant or found another boyfriend. Rylan had boy friends who cared a great deal about her.

Somehow, tonight, that wasn't as much of a consolation as it had been all those years ago.

"I'm fine, Del. I really am," she said around the lump that had formed in her throat.

Rylan pulled the door open and hurried inside the car. She started the engine and backed out of the spot as quickly as she could and drove away. The fact that distance did absolutely nothing to stop the furious embarrassment she felt meant nothing, compared to the undeniable arousal that swirled in her stomach as she'd stood close to her best friend's brother.

5

*S*he wasn't going to show.

Del felt like an idiot sitting in the booth at Margie's for the past half hour waiting for MercedesGirl926.

The booth in the back by the window was "his spot" as all of the waitresses and the owner, Margaret Madison and her daughter Kay, knew. It was done through no request of his, but since Del and the guys had started coming to Margie's as one of their few weekly excursions while staying at the House, the table held special memories for them. Margie's had also been one of the first places Del had come upon his return to Providence. The beef stew tasted so much like his mother's that he ordered it at least twice a month. And Del ordered dinner from Margie's a lot. So much that Ms. Margie had begun calling the bar every evening around five to check for his dinner order. As Del usually kept extremely late hours and the diner was open twenty-four hours a day, his order would be ready at whatever time he told them. He loved Ms. Margie and her staff for affording him this convenience and always paid more on his tab than was necessary.

Tonight, Del didn't have much of an appetite. He'd been

abnormally nervous about meeting a woman. As it turns out, that feeling was wasted since the woman was a no-show.

Del finished the slice of apple pie he'd ordered out of guilt for sitting there so long and emptied the glass of water. He was just about to stand and leave but hesitated to check his watch one more time. Maybe he was wrong. It could've just felt like he'd been sitting here forever. Nope. It had been forty-five minutes. With a frown he stood and was prepared to walk out of the diner, but he hadn't moved fast enough.

"Delano. You don't like the food at your own place?"

Mal Penning stood in front of Del, his tall, slim body and slouched posture the same as it had been since they were teenagers. They were sixteen when they'd had their first confrontation. On the basketball court behind the elementary school, Del's team from the House had been playing there first, but Mal thought he had more privilege than ten wayward teens. He told them to get lost. Rock, with his quick temper and powerful fists, had stepped in Mal's face first, demanding that he make them move.

Del, seeing how the scenario would play out—Rock would beat the crap out of Mal and Mal would call his father who was the District Attorney at the time, send the cops and put Rock in jail for a good portion of his yet to come adult life—stepped between them. Del's level-headed suggestion had been for them to play for the right to stay. Mal had laughed. He'd called them a bunch of delinquents and acted as if his group of more affluent friends didn't have the time to be bothered and attempted to walk away. Del had stepped forward, tapping Mal on the shoulder. When Mal turned Del thrust the ball into Mal's chest and stated his terms again. Mal, still needing to save face in front of his friends, had looked Del in the eye with pure contempt before saying, "You're still a broke nobody with a whore for a mother who can barely pay the rent, that's why you and your brother have to live in a house using my dad's tax dollars to take care of you and the rest of your delinquent crew."

Before Del could blink he'd punched Mal in the face, breaking the racist bastard's nose. That act had earned Del another six months at the House and made him and Mal sworn enemies. Fifteen years later and the animosity between them was still as thick as the summer air in Providence.

"Good evening, Mal," Del said and attempted to walk around the man.

They had nothing to say to each other. Too many years and too many events had happened between them for any sort of truce to ever be discussed. And Del didn't want to discuss one, especially not since Mal had been lurking around the bar for the past couple of weeks, no doubt looking for something to harass them about. Mal still thought he was better than Del for basic and idiotic reasons like race, financial position and social status. Age-old issues, that some thought were in the past. Del and his friends knew differently.

"Don't walk away from me," Mal said as he moved to block Del's path.

Del glared at him, staring into the coldest green eyes he'd seen in a very long time.

"You waltz back into my town after screwing up with the DEA and think you own things here. Well, you're wrong," Mal said.

Del shrugged. "You'd be the one who's wrong. I own two houses and part of a remarkably successful bar and grill. I'd say that's a few things that I own."

"You're still trash!" Mal insisted.

"And you're still a jealous little prick. Good to know we're clear on that."

Del once again tried to leave. This time Mal poked a finger

into his shoulder. All the rage that had bubbled in the fifteen-year-old Del bubbled in his gut and his fists clenched at his side.

"I'm gonna get you and your convict buddies out of my town if it's the last thing I do."

Del still stared at the spot where Mal's finger had touched him. Realizing that he was a grown man now, with responsibilities and people who depended on him to walk a straight line, he lifted his gaze slowly to meet Mal's and spoke with lethal clarity, "That lump in your nose should be a daily reminder of what happened the last time you tried to step to me, Mal. . So, I'm gonna advise you back the hell up and let me leave without having to break my foot off in your ass this time."

Mal flushed but just like years ago, he didn't back down. "You can't talk to me like that."

"Too late," Ms. Margie said as she joined them. "Now you know I don't take kindly to no foolishness in my place. And it would be an awful shame if I call Cannon from the newspaper and have him come down here to write the story of our esteemed City Council President harassing one of our respected business owners."

Mal ignored Margie's threat and shook his head. "You think your charm works on everybody," he told Del. "But we both know how that turns out in the end. You weren't charming enough to save her life, were you?"

Del remained silent, his teeth clenching so hard he thought he might cause some serious damage. But he wouldn't respond. He wouldn't give Mal the satisfaction of seeing him get emotional about a situation that had long since been reconciled.

"Sit down and order some food or walk out of here right now, Mal. I mean what I say," Ms. Margie insisted.

She was a short woman, with a stout posture, her thick hands planted on her hips, face fixed in a frown.

"I know what you did," Mal said. "I know and everybody else

is gonna know the minute you take the stand and testify. Your time here is almost up."

Del still didn't speak. He watched Mal walk away, tamping down on the urge to run after him and beat the hell out of him, as he started to do fifteen years ago.

"I don't have that nonsense in here," Ms. Margie was saying.

"I'm sorry," Del told her. "It wasn't my intention."

"Oh no," Ms. Margie continued with a shake of her head, her silver curls moving with the motion. "Not your fault. That boy's been a pain in the ass all his life. Parents spoiled him rotten so he thinks his shit don't stink. But I'm not afraid of him or his parents."

Del looked at her and had to smile. Margaret Madison wasn't afraid of anyone. Del really liked her.

"I'll just head out. Don't want your other customers to be uncomfortable," he told her.

"Nonsense. Sit down and eat some food. I know you had that pie, but I also know you're probably hungry. I'll get you that turkey sandwich you like and you can take it home with you."

Del wanted to tell her no, but he knew better. There was no turning down food when Ms. Margie was offering.

He sat down and scrubbed his hands over his face. This night wasn't turning out the way he'd planned.

What the hell was she doing?

It would've been more beneficial if Rylan had asked that question three weeks ago when she first began the private chats with Del. The entire situation had been ridiculous. She was too old to engage in dirty talk with a stranger over the internet. And she should've been smarter. But truth be told, she was lonely.

Sure, she had Camy and they still hung out a lot since neither of them were involved in a committed relationship. And her mother loved for her to come over for dinner or just a visit because it gave her more time to complain about what Rylan wasn't doing to be more like Naomi. And Rylan spent time with her father for sometimes more than twelve hours a day at the body shop. So it wasn't that she was totally alone in the world. She was just lonely.

And that had never occurred to her before the chatting with Del began.

Delano Greer. She despised him right about now. Half an hour ago she'd deleted his number from her phone and unconnected with him on the social networking app. She didn't want anything to do with him on the anonymous personal level. Did that mean she wanted to deal with him on a real personal level instead?

Hell no! He was Camy's brother.

But his naked chest had made her mouth water. The things he'd written to her and the way she imagined he would sound saying them, had made her panties damp with desire. It was all surreal and it was making the already stressful situation she was dealing with worse because she really needed to focus on saving the body shop. Not on daydreaming about Del Greer's body!

Rylan walked into Margie's determined to let Del know exactly how she felt about his little prank. Her conscience wouldn't let her walk away quietly. It was a curse Rylan was certain she'd inherited from her mother. If she felt she'd been wronged, she wasn't going to be satisfied until the person who wronged her either paid for what they did, or at the very least was confronted. That was her formula for closure. But the first thing she saw as she walked in the direction where the waitress had told her Del was sitting, was Del and Mal toe-to-toe. On instinct she'd begun walking in their direction, fully prepared to break up whatever was going down between the two. Ms. Margie beat her to the punch.

Rylan watched as the older woman handled both men with the stern finesse she was known for and had felt a bit in awe at the process. Margie Madison was not one to be played with, and everyone in Providence knew this. She was a strong Black woman who'd been dealt some tough blows in life, including the beating death of her parents who were attending a Civil Rights march when she was twelve, losing her firefighter husband in a warehouse fire, and then having her family home in Richmond destroyed by a random tornado a few years ago. She'd survived it all and never stopped going or teaching the next generation of Black women. Rylan was more than a little impressed with her.

That could be why she'd hung back as Ms. Margie spoke to Del privately. He'd looked like he was ready to explode with rage as Mal had stood so close—no doubt antagonizing him the way he always did. Whatever Ms. Margie said to Del had him relaxing a bit and sitting back on the red nylon covered booth seat. All while Rylan stood in the middle of a group of tables where customers were eating or wondering what the hell was going on with her.

Margie's was never empty. No matter what time of day or night Rylan came into this place, or the time of year, there were always customers sitting in the retro-themed diner, listening to the sounds of Motown and other old school R&B songs while they dined on delicious southern cooking. The Temptations' *Ain't Too Proud to Beg* was playing at the moment and Rylan used the familiar upbeat song to reinforce her courage.

"Hey," she said when she finally approached the booth where Del sat.

He was folding a straw into tiny pieces and then pulling it apart with enough force to snap it in half. But at the sound of her voice he looked up and let out a sigh.

"Hey," he replied.

"I saw Mal." She eased into the booth seat across from him without invitation.

"And he was still in one piece," Del said, his voice deep and deathly slow. "Don't know how much longer that's gonna last if he keeps flappin' off at the mouth."

He'd discarded the pieces of the last straw and pulled another one from the canister at the end of the table.

"This is an old routine," Rylan told him. "You know he's all talk. Just trying to get under your skin."

Del nodded but kept his focus on the straw. "I know all the right things. I've done all the right things. Stayed out of trouble after going to the House. Went to college, started a career. I sent money home to my mom to help with the house and my sister. And he's still got a problem with me."

"*His* problem. Not yours," she said.

He shook his head and then dropped the straw staring down at it like he was wondering what the hell he'd been doing. Then he sat back heavily against the seat and shrugged.

"You're right," he said. "Shouldn't let him get to me."

"No. You shouldn't." She paused and then opened her mouth to say something else, only to close it just as quickly. Del was an incredibly attractive guy. He wore a cream-colored shirt, short-sleeved, so the sinewy muscled arms were on display. His black hair was cut low, the beard and mustache neat and sexy. When they were teenagers, he and Lance had their left ear pierced. Lance had since added a piercing to his other ear and wore two diamond studs daily. While Del never wore an earring anymore. He rarely ever smiled either. She wondered why she'd never noticed that before.

"What are you doing here? You said you were heading home when I saw you last," he said, his deep voice interrupting her thoughts.

It was just as well. They were thoughts she definitely shouldn't have been having.

"I was hungry," she replied.

He shook his head. "You always did eat like you belonged on the wrestling team instead of under the hood of a car."

"Starving is underrated," she quipped.

The waitress showed up at that moment, handing Del a bag. He accepted it and said, "Add whatever she orders to my tab."

The woman nodded and pulled a notepad from the front pocket of her apron. She looked at Rylan with a smile that asked for her order.

"Ah, I need a few minutes to look at the menu." She wasn't really hungry.

"You want a bacon double cheeseburger with everything, mustard instead of mayo and an order of fries with salt and pepper, no ketchup," Del said dryly when the waitress was gone.

The fact that he knew her standing order at the diner was like another poke of the red-hot needle of embarrassment. It was also effective in reminding her why she'd really come to Margie's tonight—to tell Del what an ass he was for tricking her.

"Not tonight," she snapped.

"Oh really? What makes tonight any different than the last twenty years? You love cheeseburgers almost as much as you love tinkering with cars."

He'd said it in such a matter-of-fact way that she'd almost agreed with him. Except she knew it was an insult. The girls Del went out with ate like rabbits, nibbling on salads or sipping on soups as if those items actually left their belly full. They laughed at his corny jokes and batted their long eyelashes when he ran up to them on the sidelines after a game. While it had taken years for Rylan to realize that didn't make them bad people, it just wasn't the type of woman she was meant to be. Which confirmed the fact that she and Del were never going to be an item.

"I'm here because I have something to say to you," she started with determination.

Her arms had been resting on the table up to this point, but now she pulled them back, so that her hands fell in her lap.

"Say it," he prompted. "'Cause I'm heading home. It's been a really long day and I'm ready to unwind."

She nodded. "With a beer and your newspaper?"

He blinked and then shrugged. "Yeah, probably. I don't know. I might just toss this sandwich into the fridge and crash."

"Really? What about getting online?"

"What? Why would I get online at this time of night?"

It was her turn to shrug. "I don't know. You may be looking for someone...I mean expecting to hear from someone online."

He didn't respond but continued to stare at her.

It was now or never and she really shouldn't feel anxious about saying what needed to be said. This whole situation was his fault, not hers. She took a deep breath and released it slowly.

"For instance, maybe you were sitting here tonight expecting to see MercedesGirl926. And because she obviously didn't show up, now you're going to head home, sit in your favorite chair by the window in your bedroom and pull out your phone. What will you say, "Missed you tonight?" Or maybe not, since, as it turns out, she did actually show up." Her words stopped then, although her heart continued beat rapidly.

She lifted her arms again, this time folding them on the table as she leaned in to look closer at Del.

"I showed up to meet GCSports18 face-to-face," she said and waited for his smart-ass response.

But it didn't come.

Instead, a look she could only attribute to stark terror crossed Del's face. His eyes widened, his lips parting as if he wanted to say something and then snapping shut as he began to shake his head.

"What? You didn't think I was going to figure it out?" She

huffed. "Well, I'll admit I may not have, at least not for a while. But your bestie was kind enough to share your screen name with me tonight at the bar. So now I know."

"You…know…what?" he asked, that ridiculous look of shock still plastered on his face.

"I know that you're GCSports18. Or rather, you're the big fat idiot who thought it would be cool to play another sordid joke on me. Even though we're both grown and too damn old for your antics! Was Lance in on this too? Of course, he was, you're twins and this is your niche."

"Rylan, I don't know what you're talking about."

"Oh, you know exactly what I'm talking about," she said and then stood. "And I came here tonight to tell you to cut it the hell out! This was by far your cruelest joke yet. Making me…getting me to send you that picture and then…," She paused because she couldn't actually say the rest. She'd thought she was prepared to really let him have it, but the way he was looking at her, the churning of her stomach now that she was confronting him, and the stupid shaking of her hands, had her ready to bolt.

"Just stop it!" she continued. "I'm not going to be the butt of your jokes anymore."

Rylan did walk away at that point, but she did it slowly and as normally as she could manage. She wasn't running from Del or the embarrassment he'd made her feel. She was leaving him to stew in the fact that she'd found him out. And for a minute she'd thought she made a grand escape. She was halfway to her car when she felt his hand on her elbow, turning her to face him.

"What the hell are you saying?" His question coupled with the intent look on his face was more like a command.

"You heard what I said," she countered and yanked her arm free of his grasp. Even though the warmth from the spot he'd touched had already begun to spread.

He was shaking his head again. "You're MercedesGirl926?"

She stepped to the side and pointed at her car. "Mercedes."

With both hands she gripped her breasts, a gesture she would later question. "Girl."

"And my birthday is September 26th," she told him as if her identity was a no-brainer.

It was then that she noticed his gaze had fallen to her breasts, which coincidentally were still being palmed. She immediately pulled her hands away and propped them onto her slim hips.

"Look, I'm not amused by this joke, Del. How could you do that to me? Whose idea was it to make me do those things and why did you think it was funny? It was cruel and—"

"Whoa. Wait a minute." He took a step back, holding his hands out in front of him as if he thought she was going to move closer to him. "Stop. Just stop."

She didn't say another word because he actually looked as if he were ready to pass out. He'd stopped shaking his head as if the disbelief was finally wearing off, leaving what in its place? And why the hell wasn't he laughing? That's what she'd expected him to do.

"I didn't do those things," he said.

"Really, Del? That's your defense? You're going to stand there and deny it, even after Rock told me your screen name?"

"No," he said, and then went back to shaking his head. "I mean, yes. Look, I didn't know it was you. I had no idea that you were the one I was chatting with. Dammit! I knew I hated social media for a reason! Dammit!"

Wait.

He was serious.

Rylan knew the Greer twins very well, almost as well as she knew her own blood sister. They were guilty of doing a lot of things in their time but lying wasn't one of them. Whatever they did, in the end, Lance and Del always owned up to it. That's the way they were raised. She took a step back now, grateful for her reliable car that caught her from falling to the ground with dread.

"You didn't know you were talking to me and I didn't know I was talking to you," she said quietly.

"No," he replied in a similarly quiet tone. "I would have never."

"I know," she hurried to say because her embarrassment had now morphed into mortification. "Because you would've never talked to me that way. I know. Or I should've known."

She was so not Del's type. Had never thought she wanted to be his type. This was a mess.

"Okay, look," she said and then paused to take a deep breath. She rubbed her trembling hands down her thighs and summoned the courage to continue. "It was a fluke. A misunderstanding. No need for us to make it any bigger. We'll just walk away and forget it ever happened."

Forget that the best orgasm she'd ever brought herself had been because of Del's bare chest.

"You don't tell anybody and I won't tell anybody. That's it. Done," she finished. "Deal?"

Del nodded, still looking a bit dumfounded.

"Deal," he said.

"Good. Deal. I'm ah, I'm just gonna go home now."

And die a slow and mortified death.

"Yeah. Me too," he replied.

"Yeah. Okay, so good night," Rylan said and then for the second time tonight, hurried to get into her car and drive away from Del Greer.

6

*T*he orange light on the console glared back at him. Del sat behind the wheel of his truck and stared at it. He needed an oil change. Normally, he would pull the truck into his driveway and spend a few hours handling the task himself. He was no mechanic, but there were some basic things he knew how to do and he was very particular about who he let touch his truck. There weren't many things that Del was protective of—outside of blood-related family and the brothers—but his truck was one of them.

Which was why as soon as the traffic light on the corner of Penn Street changed, he lifted his foot from the brake and made a right turn down Linthicum Lane. Two blocks later, Del made another right turn onto the lot of Kent Automotive.

He'd taken his truck to one other mechanic since he'd purchased it in D.C., but Del wasn't about to drive all the way back there to have his oil changed. No, it was probably time to find a new mechanic. This just happened to be the most reputable place in town.

It wasn't because he wanted to see Rylan again.

They were into the first week of December now. Temperatures had dropped significantly and the town looked like a page out of one of those Christmas movies Camy loved watching. There was even a wreath hanging on the front door of the body shop, and garland stretched around the two automatic doors that led to the work bays. After parking his truck, Del walked to the door and entered the building, heat blasting his face the moment he stepped inside. There was also jazz music filtering loudly throughout the reception area where there should've been a receptionist or someone to greet him or offer assistance. Since there wasn't, Del crossed the industrial carpeted floor. He pushed through the swinging door and walked down the ramp leading into the open garage space. He knew this place well as Mr. Will had been the only one able to keep Del's first car—a royal blue '68 Chevy Camaro—running back in the day.

The area seemed bigger now, tools lining part of one wall, tires stacked neatly in rows on the other side of the building and in between a host of other electronic and manual equipment. There were also two cars in the bay area, one already on the lift and the other with a great ass sticking out from beneath the hood.

Her jeans were ripped in strategic places, one being the left back pocket, but not all the way through so that he could see what she was wearing beneath the denim. The material hugged her long legs like a glove, perfectly outlining the roundness of her ass and the thighs he'd thought about multiple times via the picture saved on his phone.

But he hadn't come here to see her.

It had been four days since that night at the diner where she announced their colossal mistake. And Del had needed a moment to recoup. Rylan hadn't come into the bar during that time. For that Del was grateful because he wasn't certain how he would react around her after jerking off to the picture of her one bare leg.

Now, he knew.

His dick grew harder than any one of the tools in this whole damn garage.

"Hey, Rylan," he said when he felt like a total jerk just standing there gawking at her.

She moved slowly, easing up and then back, before turning to face him. She had a torque wrench in one hand, a dirty cloth in the other. Her gray t-shirt had seen better days, between smudges of dirt and oil and the rip on the right shoulder, but it still managed to look sexy. Today, her hair was pulled back into a messy sort of ponytail and her face was completely free of make-up. She looked far better than any woman Del had ever seen.

"What are you doing here?" she asked after the first few stunned moments of silence.

"I have a problem that only you can solve," he said.

She arched a brow and leaned back against the car she'd been working on.

"I told you this is no longer funny, Del. Don't come to my place of business with your little juvenile antics." Her tone was icy, her gaze fierce and her stance was unbothered. Sexy. Sexy. And the sexiest.

He almost groaned.

"I'm serious. I need an oil change and you're the only one I trust to touch my...uh, my truck," he finished after struggling with his wandering train of thought.

This was insane. He'd told himself this every day since that night at Margie's. He couldn't be attracted to Rylan Kent. There was no way. He'd known her forever. He'd seen her wearing pajamas and hair rollers and almost falling down the stairs as she tried to walk in heels when going to her first school dance. In all those years, he'd never thought of her as anything other than a little sister. In the past four days he'd thought of her constantly and not in a way that any brother should think about his sibling.

"Again, don't play with me, Del. I know you've been tending to your own precious truck since you came back to town. Why bring it to me now? And for just an oil change?" Her eyes narrowed as she asked that question, meaning she didn't believe a word he'd said.

"The weather's changed," he argued. "I figured in addition to the oil change you could do a complete maintenance check. You know, like your sign out front says, "Be prepared for Old Man Winter, Get Your Vehicle Serviced Now!" I don't want to take any chances especially since Ms. Margie's arthritis has predicted a long hard winter for us."

Everything he'd just said was true. He only left out the part where there were two other body shops and a Cadillac dealership in Providence. He could have easily gone to one of them. But he'd come here. Going anywhere else had never crossed his mind.

Because he wanted to see Rylan.

"Fine," she snapped after a moment of contemplation. "Leave the key in that box over there. I have two before you, but I should get to it by the end of the day. I'll call if there's any issues, otherwise be here by 7 to pick it up."

She turned away from him then, once again leaning under the hood of the other car. Del stood there staring for a few moments before realizing—for the first time in his life—he didn't know what else to say. He knew what he was feeling at the moment, lust so thick and potent that it threatened to choke him. But he also knew what was at stake. She was his sister's best friend and a pretty important person in his life as well. Sex—or rather, more sex than they'd already experienced together—would only complicate their existing relationship. And truth be told, it could ruin it. Del had some experience with ruining relationships with women, so he didn't doubt that.

He should just walk away. Keep today's interaction purely professional. That was the smart thing to do. Del hadn't done too many smart things in the last two years and he'd vowed to change that. So, he took his own advice and turned away from the delectable view that Rylan was inadvertently offering. He dropped his keys into the box as instructed and left the body shop. And because he hadn't really thought his plan of stopping by for an oil change through thoroughly, he zipped his leather jacket and pulled out his gloves as he prepared to walk the three and a half blocks to Camy's so he could get her to drive him to the bar.

The cold air and brisk pace in which he walked would do him good. It would cool down the heat that infused his body whenever he thought about Rylan and that thigh pic she'd sent him.

Or at least it should have.

Del cursed as he stopped, waiting to cross the street, because walking in the cold with a hard dick wasn't the most comfortable form of exercise.

***

"Whose fancy truck is that?"

Rylan startled as her father's voice echoed throughout the bay area. William Barton Kent had a thick booming voice that went perfectly with his tall, brawny build. He was wearing his usual dark gray jumpsuit with Kent Automotive written in white script over the left breast pocket. It was a well-worn outfit that matched the scuffed black boots he wore. His salt and pepper colored hair was cut low to his scalp, the beginnings of a similarly colored beard sprouting at his chin. There was no other man Rylan had ever loved.

"It's Del's," she answered without looking up.

Rylan was almost finished replacing the thermostat in the Grand Marquis that she'd been working on for the past hour. Had she not taken a twenty-minute break after Del's departure to gather her wits, she would've already moved on from her first task of the day. She wanted to hurry up and get to his truck, so that he could come back and pick it up and she could be done with seeing him.

Who was she kidding? Providence wasn't big enough that she'd never see Del again. Besides, he was Camy's brother...no, Rylan was tired of going around and around that point. She knew who Del was and all the reasons why he wasn't the man for her. She just had to figure out how to accept it.

"I wondered when he'd finally get around to bringing that beauty in here," Will said as he grabbed a couple of buckets and towels. He went over to the second half of the loading bay and circled the Buick that was waiting there.

"It's just an oil change," she told her father.

"Well, check everything out. Those Cadillacs have a list of problems that people don't know about until they've already spent a bundle buying them," he warned.

"I know, Dad," she said and stood up. She grabbed the towel that she'd stuffed in her back pocket and wiped her hands. "I'll do a full check, just as soon as I take care of the Ford parked out front. And then I want to give Lamborghini Guy another call."

Will made a grumbling sound. "Asshole," he said finally. "In thirty days, we're selling that car, just like our service agreement says. And then we're filing suit against him for non-payment. We're not a parking garage, nor do we offer free services."

"I know, Dad," Rylan repeated. But she'd much rather get the money Lamborghini Guy owed them than to go through the paperwork and subsequent hassle of filing a lawsuit.

Even if they sold the car, her father would give her half the proceeds, just as they'd been splitting the proceeds of the shop for the last few years. With her share of the sale, Rylan would definitely be able to afford the down payment on the loan to buy the business. It was an option she was strongly considering, but first, she wanted to exhaust all methods of contact.

A few minutes passed while Rylan continued cleaning the area where she'd been working. She closed the hood of the Grand Marquis and was just about to slip behind the driver's seat to start the engine and double-check her work, when her father spoke again.

"I'm gonna sell the place and give your mother the money I owe her," he said stoically. "It's the right thing to do."

Rylan froze.

"It was your retirement fund. Not hers," she told him.

She'd been thinking this for a few weeks but hadn't wanted to get into it with her father or her mother. Now, she didn't see a choice.

"If you die before her, she'll be able to claim your social security benefits. And she has her own pension from the school system. In addition to the retirement fund she started for herself. I'd say she's going to be in pretty good financial condition when this divorce is over."

Will shook his head. "I owe it to her."

"Dad—" Rylan started to say, but her father dropped one of the buckets.

The sound was loud and cut off her words.

"I owe it to her." Will insisted. "I made vows and promises to her when we married and I broke them. I should've never gambled away that money. I have to make amends."

"You don't have to do anything. If you're tired of running the shop, just say that. But don't let her guilt you into selling just because she wants more money," Rylan said and meant every word.

She felt her mother was being unfair and that her father's guilt was making him lay down and take whatever Estelle and her lawyer dished out. Rylan wasn't having it.

"Sell the place to me," she said. "You can do what you want

with the proceeds, even though I think paying her off is a mistake. But I want to keep the shop."

"No," he said simply. "It's deep in debt and too much for you to handle on your own. You should find yourself a good husband, go off and start a family. I don't want you burdened with my mistakes too."

He'd come to stand in front of the Grand Marquis. Rylan sat there for quiet moments just staring at him. He looked old and tired. When had that happened? There were wrinkles at the corners of his eyes and his almond brown skin looked ashen. Had he lost weight? After leaving the house he'd worked so hard to pay for, her father had moved in with his brother who lived in an old farmhouse just off the interstate. She'd driven out there on Thanksgiving after having dinner with her mother, Naomi and Ellis.

He moved, coming around to the driver's side of the car where she sat with the door propped open. Squatting, he reached out a hand and touched her shoulder.

"I shouldn't have let you hang around here so much. You've got more potential than I ever had and you could do more with your life." He sighed. "I've always wanted the best for you and your sister. I made some really bad mistakes and I can't undo them. But I can start to make smarter moves. I have to, Rylan."

He was telling her to let this go. To walk away from the only place she'd ever really felt like she belonged. Rylan didn't know if she could do that.

It was late afternoon before Rylan was able to pull Del's truck into the bay. She was hungry and had a headache. She wanted to go home and lay down, to clear her mind. She wanted none of this to be happening.

"This" included the situation with Del.

How had she gotten herself in this mess with him? She never chatted personally with anyone online. Why now? And why him, of all people?

And on top of that, she hadn't been able to get him out of her mind even after she'd found out who he really was. The dream that awakened her this morning was proof.

Del had let her take the lead and Rylan began by touching him. Inch by inch of gorgeous dark chocolate hued skin, the stretch of muscles and chiseled planes of his chest, abs and limbs. Her hands seemed small and frail as they traveled the expanse of his body, touching every part of him to ensure that he was real. That the desire she felt deep down in her bones for him was real.

He lay on her full-size bed, his six-foot two-inch frame seemingly too big for the mattress. Yet he was stretched out against her pale blue sheets, his hands tucked behind his head, eyes half closed as he watched her. She should've been intimidated by that look and the heat she could feel pouring from his glare, but she wasn't. Instead, she'd felt empowered.

Moving again, she straddled his waist with a quick scream of her thigh muscles as they stretched to accommodate the motion. Flattening her palms over his broad chest she leaned forward and touched her fingers gingerly to one of his puckered nipples. He didn't move. His sinewy build remained calm even as her heart beat a rampant rhythm.

She kissed the other nipple while her hand moved over the former pectoral and gripped it mildly. He smelled so good. Vaguely like the cologne he'd probably sprayed earlier that day, but more like man, masculine and delicious. Her mouth watered and her center pulsated. Moving down his chest, Rylan continued to taste his smooth skin while feeling his taut muscles. Until she came to his thick erection.

Her first reaction was to stop and stare. At his length and

girth, the heavy sac beneath and the muscled thighs to each side of it. An eerie hunger churned in the pit of her stomach, something she'd never experienced before and once again her mouth watered. She wanted to take him into her mouth. To suck him deep into the back of her throat. But first she needed to touch him.

Rylan's narrow fingers wrapped around his thick length and she briefly prayed he couldn't feel her calloused skin against his. Lifting her gaze, she saw that his hands had come from behind his head and he was now staring at her with a look of pure lust on his face. She moved her hand up the length of his dick, running her thumb lightly over its bulbous tip. He made a low groaning sound and Rylan licked her lips. She continued to work her hand over him, loving the feel of his hardness and the warm drops of pre-cum that seeped from his tip.

Del was actively moaning now. He still didn't move, but there was no doubt that he was enjoying her ministrations.

"Now," he growled when she grasped his balls, massaging them between her fingers. "In your mouth, right, fucking now."

The guttural command sent shivers of pure pleasure through Rylan's body. She immediately leaned forward, opened her mouth over the head of his cock and…

She woke up.

Her nightgown had been twisted up around her stomach, the material sticking to her sweaty skin. Her panties were drenched in both sweat and desire. She sat up in the center of her bed, breathing as if she'd just run a marathon. Her breasts felt full and heavy, her mouth, still wet as her pussy throbbed with need.

She'd known she was lost as she rolled out of the bed and headed straight for the shower. She shouldn't have been dreaming about Del. Not in a sexual way and definitely not in such vivid detail. He wasn't attracted to her in that way. Not now that he knew who MercedesGirl926 really was. And dreaming that things were different was stupid and a waste of time.

That's what she'd been telling herself for the past four days. That she was delirious with stress about possibly losing the shop and that's why she was even entertaining anything so ludicrous with Del. But then he'd waltzed his fine ass into her garage. *Her space.* And he'd stood there looking at her as if nothing had happened between them, as if he hadn't been haunting her dreams on a daily basis. She'd wanted to punch him in his smirking face. Only he wasn't smirking. He'd simply talked business and stared at her.

Could he see that her body was still reacting to his proximity? That the moment she'd seen him standing there she'd envisioned him naked and lying in her bed as he'd been in her dream? Did he somehow know how much she wanted him to make love to her?

No. Absolutely not. Because then he really would've had a good laugh.

Rylan shook her head. She grabbed his keys and moved his truck into the bay and positioned it on the lift. In the next hour she forced herself to focus solely on doing her job.

Moving away from the truck periodically, she used her tablet to punch in numbers and record notes about what she saw. She ran diagnostic tests, evaluated the results, bumped her head on a tire because she'd miscalculated her distance and cursed any number of times because for all the work she was doing, the fact that this was Del's truck and that he would eventually waltz back in here to pick it up, never left her mind.

Finally, when her inspection of the truck was complete, Rylan sighed heavily. Not because of the two-hour job, but because she had it bad for a guy that was so off limits it wasn't even funny.

7

"Have you noticed any strange vibrations?" Del immediately stopped his trek into the garage.

"Vibrations?" he asked cautiously.

As if she realized where his train of thought had skidded off to, Rylan turned to him slowly and cleared her throat. "In your truck. When you're driving, have you noticed it vibrating?"

It didn't matter that she'd slowed her speed of talking and was sure to clarify each word by pointing at the truck parked in the center of the bay. Del still thought about the sound of a vibrator and the sight of Rylan using one to bring herself to orgasm that night they'd been on the phone. Of course, she hadn't told him that's what she'd done, but the visual had quickly popped into his mind and thus, as it had been doing on and off for most of the day, his dick jumped with interest.

"I don't think so," Del replied and considering his growing erection began walking slowly behind her.

"Escalades are known for having chassis vibration issues, so I just wanted to check to see if you've been experiencing any shaking or vibrating while driving. But your motor mount is pretty worn down, so if you haven't been having problems, you will be soon. I can install a new mount but I'll need to order the part and it might take a couple of days. Other than that, everything else checked out fine," she said and stopped at the back end of the truck.

Del had been watching her walk…and only half listening to what she was saying. Something was going to start vibrating if she didn't take care of it in the next couple of days. Or at least that's what he thought she'd said. With heat soaring through his body at the sight of her plump ass switching in those tight jeans, Del thought he might actually begin vibrating from trying to suppress his desire.

"Del?" she yelled his name and he shook his head in an attempt to clear his thoughts.

"Yeah. Ah, how long did you say?"

"You're not listening to a word I'm saying," Rylan told him as she crossed her arms over her chest.

The motion pushed her breasts up, until Del thought for sure they would spill over the top of the V-neck collar of her t-shirt. He was really losing it. He lifted a hand and with his fingers squeezed his eyes shut and rubbed the bridge of his nose. He cleared his throat before opening his eyes again and tried once more to look at her in a purely friendship/professional nature.

He failed dismally.

Her lips were pouty, free of any type of gloss or color and kissable. She had high cheekbones and lovely arched brows that he was almost certain were natural.

"I hear what you're saying, Rylan," Del told her. "But to be quite honest, I'm having a hell of a time making any sense of it."

She shrugged and shook her head. He could agree, he was confused as hell by what was going on here as well.

"Look, here's the deal. I can't stop thinking about you. About all that we talked about during those chats. The daily business stuff *and* the other stuff." And it was definitely a combo of both. While today thoughts of desire seem to pump through his veins like he was receiving some type of intravenous dose of her all damn day long, last night he fallen asleep thinking about a conversation they'd had about running a business. She was smart, giving him great suggestions that he'd already implemented at the bar. How he'd missed this side of Rylan all this time still baffled him.

"But it was a mistake," she said after taking a deep breath and exhaling with a huff.

"Yes," he agreed. "It was. I had no idea I was chatting with you and you had no idea you were chatting with me. But the fact is, we were chatting with each other. We were talking to each other about what we liked sexually and how we liked it. And now all I can see when I close my eyes, or think when I open them, is how I would've killed to see you lying on your bed that night touching yourself until you came."

To her credit, Rylan didn't gasp at his blunt words. To Del's ears they sounded a bit crass, but he couldn't help it. They were exactly what he was thinking and had been feeling in the past few days. She did take a step back, her arms falling to her sides to grip the bumper of the truck.

Del sighed. He ran a hand down the back of his head and wished like hell he wasn't feeling this way. But he'd never been one to lie to anyone, least of all himself.

"Look, I know it's awkward and if you're not feeling the same, then that's cool. I'll pay you whatever is necessary to fix the truck and stay out of your way. But—"

"But what?" she interrupted and then licked her lips.

Del almost groaned. *Almost.* He managed to keep it together, kind of. "But if you're feeling this torturous heat that won't let you eat or sleep, that keeps pressing against every part of your body demanding relief, all you have to do is say the word."

She tilted her head as if she were actually considering what he'd just said. "And then what?"

He cleared his throat because the instant answer was definitely going to be a bit on the side of crude. "Then we do whatever we feel is best…to find relief…with each other." Del had never wished for a positive answer more than he did at this exact second. He wanted to hurry her thought process along by taking a step toward her. But he didn't. Crowding her, forcing her, in any way was definitely not his style. He'd wait until she came to him, or asked him to come to her, whichever came first. But he'd suffer while waiting. It was insane and he couldn't explain it but there it was.

"Our friends," she said quietly. "Our lives. Everything could be ruined."

"Or we could be great. Just one time we could give in to what we mistakenly created and I could give you pleasure. You could give me pleasure. Just one time," he stated. Or was he begging? Pride was easily out the window because he didn't take the words back. He couldn't.

"I've never looked at you this way before," she admitted. "But now, I can't stop looking at you and wondering…"

"Needing." He finished the sentence for her, knowing exactly how she felt because he'd been feeling the same way. In fact, he was struggling to resist the urge to reach out and touch her at this moment.

"Yes," she replied in a hushed whisper.

"One time, Rylan," he said and took a tentative step toward her before stopping. "Don't you want pleasure, just this once?"

She immediately nodded as if the words just wouldn't come, but at the same time, desire wasn't an option.

"Then you can have it," he said with a sigh of relief. "We can have it."

And then he could finally get her out of his system, because Del didn't like wanting something he couldn't have—not at this point in his life when he'd sacrificed so much.

"We can have it," she repeated and eased away from the truck stopping a few inches away from him.

"We can," Del said before all his control was lost and he wrapped his arms around her slim frame, pulling her close. His palms pressed against her back at the same time that his lips crashed down over hers.

She lifted her arms and wrapped them around his neck, tilting her head and opening her mouth to the warm touch of his tongue.

They were really doing this.

In the garage after hours.

Rylan was going to have sex with Del.

Well, alrighty then!

His close-cut hair felt so soft against her fingers as she held his head tightly in place while they kissed. His lips were strong, his tongue masterful as it pulled her in deeper, arousal seeping through her with every second of their embrace. Her thighs were already trembling, like she couldn't wait for this to go further even though she still couldn't believe it was happening in the first place.

"Are you sure?" she asked when the kiss was finally broken as he'd pressed her back against the truck.

His fingers were moving rapidly to pull her t-shirt from the band of her pants. In answer to her question, Del lifted her arms high above her head. He locked gazes with her and pulled her shirt up and over her head, tossing it somewhere on the garage floor. Rylan shivered as the cool air hit her heated skin. Behind the thin material of the sports bra she wore, her nipples instantly hardened. As if her body were sending him a signal, Del's gaze immediately dropped to her breasts.

"I'm damn sure," he said, his voice raspy with desire.

Her pussy clenched at his words, her breathing hitched and a feeling of power and adoration soared through her entire body. She pulled the bra up and over her head, leaving her medium-size breasts bare to him. He stared down at the twin mounds with their pebble-hard dark brown nipples and licked his lips. Damn, she loved how he was looking at her as if he'd never seen anything as pretty, or perhaps perfect. She'd never really thought of herself as a sex symbol but she knew she liked sex and had always been keen to what pleasured her. Right now, watching Del's lips part and his hands lift in a slow-motion journey to touch her breasts lightly had her gasping. He gripped them lightly and she wondered for a second if he was wondering if they were real. Of course, they were, nobody would pay money for boobs her size. Still she was proud of her B-cup tatas that were high and firm. When Del closed his eyes while closing his fingers around them and moaned, she figured he was satisfied with them as well.

Rylan took that moment to touch Del's cheek, wondering why she'd never thought of how it would feel to get her hands on him in this way. Her palm rested against his strong jaw, the tickle of his beard rubbing against her skin. He turned into her palm, touching his lips to the spot, while his hands slowly kneaded her breasts. She pressed her other hand against his chest. He wore a black leather jacket over his red Game Changers polo. She could feel the toned outline of his pecs through the material. His kisses moved to the inside of her wrist and up her arm, until his mouth had found its way to one tight nipple. She sucked in a breath the moment his tongue touched the hardened bud.

He took her nipple into his mouth with the same fervor in which he'd kissed her moments ago. She arched into him, pressing her breast further into his mouth as if she were feeding him. Why did his tongue feel so good wherever it touched her? When his teeth scraped over her nipple she gasped, her fingers digging into his shoulders. On a ragged moan she shoved at his shoulders until his mouth and hands released her breasts. With hurried motions she pushed his jacket off, vaguely hearing the muffled sound of it falling to the floor. Guided solely by need at this point, she yanked the polo and the undershirt he wore over his head and tossed them both to the floor. Now their chests were bare. Del went back to her breasts and Rylan reveled in the feel of his bare biceps beneath her fingers. He was so hard all over, from his shoulders down his arms, to the bulge of his dick she could feel as he thrust against her. She let her head lull back until it tapped the window, giving him unfettered access to her breasts while her hands familiarized themselves with every hard-sculpted inch of his upper body.

She felt like she was looking at one of those fitness magazines and imagining how the toned male bodies would feel to her touch. Now, she knew. Hot flesh over turgid muscle felt glorious. His mouth devouring one breast while his hand worked the other was like an added bonus, one that was going a long way to bringing the desire Rylan had been feeling these past few days to a boiling point.

"I want you right here. Right now." Del groaned when he pulled his mouth away from her.

His voice was deeper, his eyes darker as he looked down at her, again asking her permission. Rylan hadn't been sure how to act when he'd so blatantly told her he wanted her minutes ago, now, however, she knew exactly what she wanted.

"Then take me," she replied and let her hands fall to the buckle of his belt. "Right here. Right now."

"Yeah," he murmured and forcefully yanked the button of her jeans. "I am."

They unzipped each other's jeans simultaneously. Del pushed the material down Rylan's legs while she shimmied her hips to assist. Rylan eased Del's pants down his legs and gasped when his long hard dick slipped through the slit of his boxers to greet her. She wasted no time wrapping her hands around him, loving the feel of instant heat the contact produced. He was big and thick and her heart thumped wildly at the thought of him fitting inside her.

Del slipped a hand beneath the band of her very unpretty boy shorts. She hadn't planned on having sex today and so wasn't prepared. That was a woeful understatement because the moment his fingers eased between her legs, separating the plump folds to find the moist heat buried there, Rylan nearly jumped out of his reach with eagerness.

"I gotchu', babe," he whispered as one arm slipped around her waist to pull her close. "You just keep on touching me and I'll take care of you."

Rylan couldn't have torn her hands from his rigid length if her life depended on it. She loved the feel of him, stroking him, hearing the sounds of his hunger for her. His palm was flat against her mound now, fingers moving masterfully along her center. She leaned into him, opening her legs as much as possible considering her jeans were at her ankles and her boy shorts weren't as giving as she would have liked.

None of that seemed to matter because with each stroke of his fingers from the bud of her clit down to her throbbing opening, she fell deeper into the abyss of pleasure that was Delano Greer. He held her in his grasp so effortlessly while working her to what was going to be a ferocious orgasm in just a few moments. He wasn't doing anything special, just moving his fingers from one point to the other, spreading her desire over the sensitive warm skin, stroking the fire that had been on low heat until it scorched her soul. Rylan felt the quick tug, the shaking of her thighs and bit down on her lower lip. It was coming. Her hands grasped his dick tighter, jerking him until pre-cum covered his tip. Del leaned into her, his lips against her earlobe as he whispered, "Come for me, baby. Come all over my hand."

She did.

With a jerk of surprise and a moan of sheer pleasure, Rylan let his fingers pull from her the most intense orgasm she'd ever experienced. It was a good thing he held onto her so tightly because the moment her legs ceased shaking, Rylan was certain they would've buckled and she would tumble to the floor. Instead, she felt Del's lips on her neck, his tongue leaving a warm path across her skin.

He pulled back slowly, his face hovering just inches away from hers. Rylan couldn't help but pant, her fingers slipping uselessly from his still throbbing dick. She knew she probably looked inexperienced or delirious, but she didn't care, she felt invigorated. Del eased his hand from between her legs and out of her underwear. He lifted his fingers to his mouth and sucked her glistening essence from his fingers. Was it too soon for another orgasm?

"Delicious," he whispered. "Just as I knew you would be."

Yeah, she could melt into a useless puddle of goo right at this moment and all would be perfectly fine in her world.

But Del had other thoughts. He stepped back from where she was still standing against his truck, reaching down into his pocket until he found his wallet. Rylan heard the rustle and tear of a condom packet. The sound snapped her out of her pleasure haze and she took the condom from him. Rylan pushed Del's boxers down and worked the latex over his length. Del pushed her boy shorts down until they were in reunion with her jeans at her ankles. He leaned forward and extended a little more effort to free one of her legs from the material. As he rose back to a standing position, he brought her leg with him, locking it behind his back.

When he stepped closer again, the head of his dick pressed against the moist flesh of her pussy and she moaned.

"I've thought about being inside of you every second of every day since that night on the phone," he told her.

"Me too," she admitted. "I dreamed of you inside me."

His lips crashed over hers in that moment. His tongue thrusting deep inside her mouth, dueling with hers as if they were long lost lovers. Rylan clasped his shoulders. She held him to her as if she could somehow freeze this moment in time. Capture this very second of explicit desire and never let it go.

He positioned himself, one hand cupping the back of Rylan's head while he kissed her senseless, the other holding her ass cheek as he guided his dick to her waiting heat. Rylan moaned at the feel of his tip pressing against her entrance. She pumped against him, eager for the moment when they would be entwined. Del thrust his hips once, the tip of his engorged dick pressing past the tight barrier of her entrance. She pulled her mouth away from his and cried out in a mix of pleasure and delicious pain.

"Hold on to me," Del whispered and kissed her once more.

Rylan did as she was told. She wrapped her arms around Del's neck and held on tightly. He thrust forward again, this time inserting his full length inside her with the effort. She stretched, her muscles throbbing around his girth, and moaned.

"Damn." Del moaned too after pulling his mouth away from hers. He was holding completely still inside of her while Rylan's body begged for more.

"Rylan," he said and she opened her eyes to look at him.

"You're holding me so tightly inside and outside," he continued, letting his forehead fall to hers. "I don't know if I can stand it."

Hell, she knew she couldn't.

"Please, Del," she whispered and thrust against him. "Now."

He nodded. "Yes. Now." And he began pumping inside of her.

It was a fierce ride, the up and down adrenaline rush of a roller coaster with the unmitigated ebb and flow of a smooth melody. Del moved masterfully, his length easing in and out of her until she was chanting his name. The sound of his body slapping against hers echoed throughout the garage. She was wet and full and loving every second of it.

Yes, this was Del. This was the man who had occupied her thoughts for the last week. It was the man who was currently working his gorgeous dick deep inside of her and causing her to rethink ever masturbating again. In this moment Rylan wanted him more than she'd ever wanted anything in her life. And she was getting him, every delicious inch of him thrusting into her as if there was no place he'd rather be.

Minutes later, she trembled and disintegrated in his arms. Her second orgasm was made better only by the guttural moans from Del and his choked admission that he was coming too.

One hour after leaving the garage.

Rylan: What did we just do?

    Del: We just had a fantastic time.

    Rylan: Yeah, fantastic. And it was just this one time, right?

    Del: Right.

    Rylan: Goodnight.

    Del: Goodnight.

At three a.m., one day after Del had taken his truck to Kent Automotive and had Rylan Kent against the back of said truck, Del knocked on her door.

She lived in a three-story apartment building on the corner of Honeycomb Drive. And after texting back and forth all day and most of the evening, she'd given him the address and invited him over. Del hadn't realized how much he'd wanted that invitation. But he'd forced himself not to push. Rylan was great, but she wasn't like the other women Del had slept with. He'd known that before he'd even kissed her last night. Yet, he'd still done it.

And there were no regrets.

If he had to do it all over again, he definitely would have. It had been too good not to want more. She'd been so receptive and so in tune to what he needed at that moment. Not many words, just actions. The pulse and push of great sex. Afterward, she'd been even better than any other woman that he'd ever been with, because she'd asked no questions. As he'd gone to the bathroom to dispose of the condom and fix his clothes, Rylan had dressed. When he returned to where they'd stood by his truck, she had a printed estimate of the work that needed to be done waiting for his signature. Del signed on the dotted line and she told him his truck would be ready in a few days. She offered to drive him home, but he told her he'd gotten a rental car.

Del waited while Rylan locked up the garage and walked her to her car. He stopped her from getting in, pulling her close for a hug that some part of him knew meant more than just a "hug" should. She smiled at him and then got in the car and drove off. By the time he'd arrived home, she'd sent him the first text. A very casual exchange that despite his insistence that it had been a one-time event had him falling asleep wondering when he'd be able to enjoy her again.

Those thoughts followed Del throughout the day and well into his shift at the bar. It had invaded every second of his thoughts, until his body was tense with desire and his mind was full of a dark-hued woman with rich brown eyes and soft lips.

And now, he was waiting for that woman to open the door, the same way she'd opened the one inside of him he'd thought closed for far too long.

8

"*H*i," she said with a warm smile the moment she looked up to see him.

"Hi," Del replied and stepped into her apartment, his arms going around her waist, lips immediately finding hers.

She kissed him with the same hunger that had driven him over here tonight. It was like they couldn't get enough of each other, as her hands moved up and down his arms and his went to grip her ass. If this was how a man was welcomed home when he was married, Del was ready to go out and buy a ring and rent the church.

But Rylan eventually pulled away. She chuckled when she looked up and probably saw the quizzical look on his face. Del wasn't finished. Not by a longshot. She moved easily out of his loose grasp and went to close her door. Okay, he should've at least done that, but he couldn't think past seeing her. She put the locks in place and then walked across the room toward the couch.

"Are you hungry?" she asked as she sat, lifting her legs to cross beneath her.

A loaded question if ever Del had heard one.

"It was pretty busy at the bar tonight so yeah, I could eat," he admitted and resigned himself to being cordial.

She stood. "Well, I'm not much of a cook. But I make a fantastic grilled cheese. It's pretty late for dinner and not quite breakfast food."

He watched her walk past a small round table with two chairs in front of a window and through a doorway. His gaze traveled around to the area that served as her living and dining room. It wasn't as big as the den in his house, but it was neatly decorated with the dark blue couch she'd just moved from and rocking chair that looked like an antique, end tables, and blue and beige area rugs. The fifty-seven-inch flat screen TV mounted on the wall across from the couch was by far the focal point of the room.

"Do you prefer American or cheddar?"

Del spun around to see her peeking her head through the doorway. For a split second he saw Rylan, the teenager, looking out of the basement door at his mother's house, telling him and Lance they couldn't come down while she and Camy were there.

"Del?"

He shook his head and prayed that thought would vanish with the motion. "Yeah. Ah, you choose."

She smiled. "I love cheddar. I have a few slices of both yellow and white left, so I'll mix them. You, have a seat and turn on the TV if you'd like."

She was gone again and Del could hear her moving about in the kitchen. He thought about catching some news or finding one of the police procedurals he had a love/hate relationship with to watch. But he found himself walking into the kitchen instead. This space was even smaller. The tiled floors and backsplash a very modern light gray, stainless steel appliances and white cabinets. They were probably the updates that had sold her on this tiny place.

Rylan already had a skillet on the stove over a medium fire.

Inside, Del could see butter already melting. Her narrow fingers spread more butter on slices of bread, placing one in the skillet and then setting the other three on a paper plate. Another paper plate held slices of cheese and she layered yellow, white and then yellow over the bread in the skillet. She topped that with another slice of bread and turned to face him.

"If you're in the kitchen you can help," she told him and handed him a spatula. "Flip when I tell you."

Del shrugged and took the spatula, moving closer to the stove.

"You know what goes great with grilled cheese?"

"What?" he asked not wanting to take his gaze from the food but glancing at her anyway.

Her hair was once again pulled back into a ponytail. He wondered if he'd ever seen it all out. Rylan was not the frilly and fancy girl that Camy was. In contrast, she'd much rather slip on jeans and a sweatshirt and pull her hair back with a rubber band. Tonight, however, she wore black leggings with white snowflakes all over and a long white t-shirt that fell alluringly off one shoulder. An outfit that showed off all her feminine curves and reminded Del of just how soft she'd been in his arms.

"Hot chocolate," she continued. "And I have my own special recipe."

She was moving competently through her little kitchen, yelling "flip" just as she poured milk into a saucepan. When Del was finished with both sandwiches and had them on the paper plates she'd directed him to, he watched in awe as she opened a cabinet and stood on the tips of her toes to grab a bottle of Hennessy.

"In your hot chocolate?" he asked having never heard of this particular recipe before.

"Absolutely!" she replied. "And in yours too."

She poured a splash in the two Disney mugs she'd filled with the milk, cocoa mix, cream, sugar and vanilla. She handed him the cup with the vicious looking Scar on it and lifted hers with the lovely Princess Tiana. Reaching around him she grabbed a plate.

"Come on," she said and went to the living room again.

Del followed and sat beside her on the couch, placing his mug on the end table closest to him.

"So, was this the only place you could find in town?" Del asked and lifted half the sandwich.

Rylan had already taken a bite and slowed her chewing when he looked over to her. When she finished, she used a napkin she'd had beneath her plate to wipe her mouth.

"There's nothing wrong with my apartment," she replied. "But if you don't like it here, you're welcome to leave."

Del shook his head. "No. No. That's not what I'm saying. It's a cute little place. I'm just wondering why you moved here. Your parents' house is pretty spacious and you know Noah and Ethan renovated those lofts down by the industrial district. High ceilings, great natural light."

Rylan took another bite of her sandwich and Del did the same.

"So, you're working to lease your brothers' lofts? You guys are totally committed to each other," she said.

She sounded irritated, which was not what Del intended.

"I'm just saying, I remember how you used to practice martial arts in our basement because your mother never let you do it at your house. You have zero space to do that here."

She shrugged. "I haven't done it much lately."

"Why?" he asked and began working on the second half of his sandwich.

"Work."

Del nodded. "Yeah. I know that tune."

"What happened with you in D.C.? Why'd you leave the DEA?"

He almost choked on the bread. Another thing about Rylan, she was candid as hell.

"It was time to get out," he replied and finished chewing his food.

When she didn't say anything immediately, he knew it was because she was waiting for more of an answer. Del didn't think he had one to give.

"Fighting the war against drugs can seem pointless at times. Especially when you're on the inside of that fight," he told her and pushed the last of the sandwich into his mouth.

He wasn't hungry anymore, but he wasn't ready to leave either. And he didn't think he wanted to have this conversation.

"I can imagine," she said to his surprise. "But it was all you'd ever wanted to do. You and Lance. You played cops and robbers so much Camy and I knew you were either going to end up wearing a badge or stealing one."

When he looked at her it was to see a small smile ghosting her lips. Very kissable lips.

"It was all I thought I could do," Del told her. "Until I didn't have a choice. I couldn't do it anymore."

She nodded as if she understood that he was ending the conversation now.

"Did you enjoy the sandwich?"

"Very much," he replied and reached over to take the napkin she'd been using to wipe his mouth. "Now to try this spiked hot chocolate you made."

Del reached for the mug and took a sip. "Mmmm," he said. "This is really good. Rich and smooth. Easy going down but with just that hint of spice from the brandy."

He sat back on the couch and watched as she finished her sandwich and drank from her mug as well.

"Hmmmmm, I love it. Especially on cold winter nights." She took another sip. "Especially when it's all I have to keep me warm."

She turned to look at Del then as if she hadn't realized that she'd said that aloud. He smiled. "Well, tonight, I'm here. So, I can definitely keep you warm."

Her smile came slow, lifting her already high cheekbones and filling her eyes with a warm light. Del liked how she looked when she smiled. He liked it a lot.

"I'll bet you can," she said and took another sip.

He patted his thigh. "Come here."

She waited, watching him set his mug on the table. Del leaned forward and took the mug from Rylan's hands. He set that on the table too.

"I said, come here," he whispered before lifting her off the chair and setting her sideways on his lap.

He wrapped his arms around her and cuddled her close to his chest.

"Warm enough?" he asked.

"Definitely," she replied.

"Good." Del found the remote control between the pillows on the couch. "Now, let's see what's on late night television."

"I don't know," she said. "I'm usually asleep at this time. You know, when I'm not chatting online."

She wrapped an arm around his neck, while the fingers of her other hand ran along the edge of his jaw.

"Yeah, that online chatting is dangerous," he joked and turned on the television. "You never know what type of lunatics you might meet."

She play punched his chest and he chuckled.

He kissed her on the forehead. "And you never know what the internet might reveal before your very eyes."

Rylan tilted her head up. "Ain't that the truth," she whispered before Del kissed her lips.

———

At seven-thirty a.m., Rylan's alarm clock blared like it was pissed off at someone. The sound had her lurching up from the bed, same as every morning of her life. But she wasn't a morning person, so without the help of her trusty, but annoying as hell clock, she would always be late. After slamming her hand down over the clock, she lay back against the pillows, eyes closed and ready to steal a few more minutes of sleep. Just as she did each morning.

But the second she felt the bed shifting beside her and the hand splaying over her bare belly she realized there would be no additional sleep. Because she was not alone.

"Mornin'," Del said, his voice far too chipper at the crack of dawn.

Del was in her bed. He'd come over late last night and stayed. Wow somehow didn't cover that realization.

She should no longer be shocked at what was going on in her life. Two months ago, she'd been fine believing that she'd work at Kent Automotive for the rest of her life and continue bringing herself sexual pleasure until the moment "Mr. Right" came waltzing into Providence to sweep her off her feet. Because Rylan knew just about every guy close to her age in town and she was certain none of them were "Mr. Anything" where she was concerned.

Apparently, she'd been wrong.

"Mornin'," she replied and cleared her throat.

Her voice was very husky in the morning. Like she was a sixty-year-old man. And her hair. Damn, she hadn't tied a scarf over her hair before climbing into bed. That meant she was probably running a close look-a-like contest with Medusa right about now. And her teeth, her breath…dammit, she was not prepared for this.

But Del was.

He dropped a kiss on her shoulder, the one left bare because that t-shirt she'd been wearing when he came over was two sizes too big. Rylan didn't like shopping so when she realized she'd had the wrong size, she'd decided it would be a house shirt only, instead of dealing with going back to the store to return it. The next kiss was over the tight bud of her nipple, which felt as if it were cutting through the material of the t-shirt. After that bare skin was once again on the scene because while she'd slept the shirt had wrapped around her, rising up so that it bunched beneath her breasts.

Del kissed her torso, he moved further down and kissed her navel, pausing to look up at her.

"Was this here before?" he asked.

He was referring to the piercing. Rylan nodded. "Since our eighteenth birthdays. Camy thought it would be fun."

"I don't know about fun, but it's definitely sexy as fuck. Don't know how I missed it before."

Probably because his face hadn't been so close to her…before. And, Rylan had just changed to this particular belly ring after her shower when she'd returned from the garage yesterday morning.

He used his tongue to flick the gold Wonder Woman pendant that hung from the ruby-studded clasp of her belly ring.

"You're definitely a wonder," he whispered and continued moving lower until his breath whispered over her shaved mound.

Her leggings and panties were probably still in the living room where Del had taken them off after they'd finished their brandy-laced hot chocolate. Whose life was this?

Rylan didn't have a second to answer because Del used his fingers to part her folds and his tongue to whisper the best good morning she'd ever experienced. How did he know just where to lick and suck? And please, to every holy being, let him continue.

Her fingers gripped the sheets tightly as Rylan spread her legs wider for his assault. Del's hands were now on the back of her thighs, pushing them up into the air. She moaned and bit down on her lip until she was quite sure she would draw blood. Del kept right on licking and sucking her, the sounds he was making just as erotic as the way in which he was bringing her pleasure. He came up onto his knees and pushed her legs back further so that Rylan felt as if she were doing some sort of crazy yoga position that had her butt completely off the bed. He continued to lick and suck her with an unobstructed fervor. His tongue was everywhere, from the hood of her clit, down to a place she'd once thought forbidden.

Rylan came with a scream that probably rivaled the alarm clock. Her body shook and colors burst in a kaleidoscope behind her closed lids. Del lowered her legs then and came to lay beside her, gathering her up in his arms. He kissed her lips giving her a taste of herself as he sucked her tongue into his mouth. Rylan went with it. She wrapped her arms around him tightly, lifting a leg to circle his waist and kissed him like an almost thirty-year-old virgin—which she was not.

"Good morning," he whispered when the kiss finally broke.

She nodded. "Uh huh, good morning to you too."

It had been a very good morning until Del and Rylan stood on the sidewalk and looked at the SUV he'd rented which now refused to start.

"What are the odds?" he asked and frowned at the smoke billowing from his mouth because it was cold as Antarctica this morning.

"Apparently for you, not so good," Rylan replied. "I'll take you home and then drop you off at the bar."

"You sure?" he asked.

She looked startled by the question and then nodded. "Unless you have a better plan. I'll wait in the car while you go into your house and then I'll just drop you off at the bar. I won't go in so nobody will see us together."

"You think that's what I'm worried about?" he asked, still frowning but now for a different reason.

Rylan shrugged. Her outfit today was another pair of jeans and a black sweatshirt over a blue t-shirt. On her feet were work boots that looked way too sexy at the ends of her long legs. Her coat was a white parka with a fluffy fur hood that made her look partly like a snowman as she stood on the sidewalk.

"I know this isn't exactly what either of us planned," she said. "I'm fine with keeping it under wraps until it's run its course, I guess."

Because they weren't going to be anything other than lovers. Del could relate to that line of thought. He just didn't know how he felt about hearing her say it aloud.

"I'll be quick," he replied and began moving toward her car. When she unlocked the door, he slid into the passenger seat.

Once she climbed inside and had her seat belt on, he continued, "Only because I'm opening this morning, not because I'm rushing to get away from you."

Del was confused by the need to clear that up with her, but when she only nodded in response and started the car's engine, he simply sat back and remained silent throughout the rest of the ride.

An hour later, they pulled up in front of the bar. Del released his seat belt and was about to get out. He stopped and leaned over to touch his lips lightly to hers.

"Any man, myself included, would be lucky to have you in his life. You're not like other women, but that's a really good thing, Rylan. A really good thing."

Del stepped out of the car before she could reply. He jogged over to the door of the bar, unlocked it and slipped inside. He didn't look back, nor did he think too hard on why he'd been so bothered by her words. Did she think he was ashamed to be seen with her? Was he? And what exactly were they doing now?

This had gone past the one time they'd promised each other. Hell, he'd spent the night at her apartment, sleeping beside her in that small ass bed, holding her warm body close to his. Del had never spent the night with a woman before. Some had tried to set up those circumstances, but no matter the time or even if he'd had a drink or two, he always got up and went to his own bed. And he never invited anyone to share that bed with him. Sleeping was a solitary function for him, or at least it had been.

He'd told Rylan she wasn't like other women. Last night had proven that point. It would be good if he could reconcile with why that mattered so much to him. But it was almost ten a.m. and they were opening in an hour. Staff would be pouring in within the next half hour. He had inventory lists to go over and expense charts to review and approve. He didn't have time to stand around thinking about Rylan. But if Del were perfectly honest with himself he would admit that he would probably think of nothing else but her today.

It was becoming a habit; one he wasn't that uncomfortable with.

9

"*H*old it right there, missy!"

Rylan spun around in the parking lot, ten seconds away from lifting her arms and assuming the position as she heard the order given in a loud tone. If it weren't for the click-clack of heels on the sidewalk she would've believed she was being arrested, for what she had no idea. But she saw Camy walking confidently toward her, wearing black leather boots zipped up her calf.

"Good morning to you too," Rylan said and met Camy half-way, stuffing her hands into her coat pockets because she'd left her gloves at home.

That was most likely due to the fact that there'd been a man in her apartment this morning while she'd been getting ready for work.

"Oh no, we're skipping right past the pleasantries and getting down to the nitty gritty," Camy insisted with a shake of her head.

As of three weeks ago, Camy's hair was a honey bronze color with blonde streaks similar to the ones Rylan had in her jet-black hair. Camy's hair was styled in fluffy curls that rested on her shoulders. Today she wore black pants, the boots, and a black leather coat belted at the waist. She looked like a model with her carefully made up face and manicured nails, while Rylan burrowed into her thick coat and kept her mouth closed to keep her teeth from chattering.

"Yes, we can do this inside," Camy said, reading Rylan's mind.

She laced her arm through Rylan's and quick-walked them to the door of the body shop. Rylan entered first, with Camy hot on her heels.

"Mornin, Dad," Rylan yelled into the garage, but lead Camy in the other direction toward the offices.

"Mornin, Mr. Will," Camy yelled after her and closed the door to Rylan's office seconds after they entered.

Rylan was taking off her coat when Camy continued.

"Okay, tell me why you were dropping Del off at the bar this morning," she said before leaning her butt on the side of Rylan's desk.

Rylan had been hanging her coat on the back of the door as Camy spoke. She was grateful to not be facing her friend at the moment that question rolled out. Her motions came slower as she pulled the gray and white polka dot scarf she'd had tied around her neck and tucked under her coat, off and hung it up too.

"Stalling," Camy continued. "That means I was right to follow you here to ask questions instead of just texting you."

When Rylan turned to face Camy it was with a slight frown on her face. "You were at the bar? Why didn't you toot your horn, wave, say good morning? Something. You followed me all the way to work, which is on the opposite side of town from the school where you should be heading to teach your noon class."

Camy had always wanted to be a singer, but her mother's illness had kept her from leaving town right after high school with the talent scout that had heard Camy sing in the school talent show. After her mother's death, Camy decided that her place was in Providence, living in their family home and taking care of her brothers. For the past three years she'd taught a music class at the high school.

Camy shook her head, gold hoop earrings shaking with the motion.

"Don't even try it, missy. I want answers. Because while I know Del's truck is in your shop, I also know that he rented another SUV yesterday afternoon. I also know that from the direction you were driving, you had to be coming from Del's house and not your apartment. So, I'm asking you why."

Rylan walked around her desk. She pulled out the chair and sat down, hoping her fingers would remain steady while moving across the keyboard as she booted up her computer. She wanted to check her emails to see if Lamborghini Guy had responded to her latest round of messages.

"The rental broke down. He called to have it towed back to that shady company down on 5th Street. They rent anything to tourists, but I told Del he shouldn't pay for any repairs, or the rental and towing costs," she said as she worked to bring her computer to life.

Camy had moved from the desk, taking a seat in the brown guest chair that was a part of the same set in the waiting room.

"So instead of calling Lance or me, Del called you? Why? Because you're his favorite pseudo-sister?"

Del and Lance had called her that a lot when she was growing up because she was at their house more than she was at her own. She obviously liked being at their house more and the title they'd given her had seemed less annoying and more endearing than she supposed it should have. Until this morning. Now, hearing it made her stomach churn because the things she and Del had done last night and this morning were definitely not something siblings should do.

"Yeah," she said simply, without looking up.

Lying to her best friend wasn't something Rylan did on a regular basis. If there were anyone in this world who deserved her honesty, trust and devotion, it was Camy. They'd shared everything from their fears to their hopes and dreams, tears and laughter and everything in between. So yeah, lying to her wasn't going to work. All Rylan could hope to do was brush her off. But that wasn't so easy with a woman like Camy.

Camy made a buzzing sound as if they were on a game show. "Wrong," she snapped. "Try again and this time look at me."

Rylan's fingers still on the keyboard as she wondered how this was going to turn out. Del clearly didn't want anyone to know they were sleeping together. And really, Rylan wasn't sure she wanted to make a public spectacle of the event either. It was temporary. Clearly not one time as they'd previously planned, but neither of them were looking for anything more than good sex. And wow, were they getting that.

Ugghhh, she was not thinking that with Del's sister sitting just a few feet away.

"Rylan Sophia Kent," Camy said in a tone that meant she was definitely playing the we're-best friends-so-stop-bullshitting-me card.

Rylan sighed and spared one look at Camy before falling back in her chair. She closed her eyes and said as quickly as she could, "I slept with Del. We didn't plan for it to happen. It was sort of a fluke. Like really, on online mistake that went way too far and before we could stop it, we were having sex in the garage and then…again at my apartment last night…and this morning."

Her voice had gone from nervous and jittery to disgraced and quiet in a matter of seconds. The following silence had her peeking one eye open to see if Camy had picked up the letter opener from the mug on her desk and was coming around the desk to stab her with it. But that wasn't what she saw. Both eyes opened and Rylan sat up slowly in her chair. Camy was smiling.

"Well it's about damn time," she said with another shake of her head.

"What?" Rylan asked incredulously. "I told you we didn't plan this. It was a mistake."

"The best lessons are learned from mistakes," Camy continued. "You've been in a sexual drought for far too long and Del, well he's been in his own dark place since returning from D.C. So, this is good. It's damn good."

"I don't understand how you can say that," Rylan replied honestly and proceeded to tell Camy all the details of how she and Del came to be sex partners.

When Rylan was finished with the story, Camy laughed. And laughed.

"Girl, that is too good. It sounds like a movie with Tika Sumpter and Morris Chestnut playing the leads," she said. "I can't even imagine my brother chatting online and having phone sex!" Camy laughed some more.

"He's the uptight one of us. The very serious one, always in control of every damn thing. I wish I could've seen the two of you." Then she stopped and held up a hand. "Ah, no that may have been too much."

"Ya think?" Rylan asked, still shocked at Camy's reaction.

Was she really happy that her best friend was sleeping with her brother?

"Are you serious?" Rylan asked when Camy continued to chuckle. "I mean, this doesn't bother you at all?"

"Bother me? Why should it? Because you're my closest friend and I trust you with my life? Doesn't it stand to reason that I would also trust you with my brother's heart?" Camy asked.

Her words made sense, but it still didn't sound right to Rylan.

"Hearts aren't involved here," she replied quickly because she wanted there to be no illusions as to what was going on.

Not on Camy's part, and certainly not on her own.

"We're just kickin' it," Rylan continued. "And we're not even telling people because you know, it could end whenever." The last was said with an inconsequential wave of her hand.

Camy's laughing ceased, but her smile stayed in place. The girl-please-stop-playing smile.

"Okay, you may believe that right now because this is still new. But I know you and I know Del and neither of you are the "just kickin' it" type. That's why you've both remained single and emotional entanglement free for so long."

"Camy, no. That's really not how it is. I am not trying to hook Del. I'm just…just…" Rylan couldn't think of the words.

"You're just getting your thing off?" Camy asked and chuckled. "That's cool. But when the hot and sweaty glow of great sex wears off—because honey you are absolutely glowing this morning, even dressed in those drab ass clothes. But when that wears off, you're gonna find that hearts tend to do what they want, regardless of what the brain insists."

"Not for me," Rylan said sternly. "I'm not in this for any happy ever after. Fairy tales are definitely for you and Naomi. I'm the realistic one."

"So realistic people don't deserve love and happiness?"

Rylan shook her head. "Oh no. I'm realistic, not cynical. I'm certain I'll get married at some point and I'll have a family which will hopefully be happier than the one I was born into. But I don't believe in some sweeping tale of love where the most unlikely people in the world realize they can't live without each other and defy all the odds to be together. That's just not me."

Camy's response had been more laughter. Until Rylan had shooed her out of her office. Her friend had left after giving Rylan a tight hug and saying, "I love you even though I swear you can be the blindest and most stubborn person in all the earth."

Rylan accepted the hug and admitted her love for her friend, especially after hearing that Camy wasn't angry about what she'd done with Del. That had relieved some of the stress about what was going on between the two of them. The rest—which included how Del had looked when she'd offered to drop him off at work and the words he'd said before getting out of her car—still had her puzzled. But Rylan pushed those thoughts out of her mind and decided to focus on work, because that was the one thing she could control right now. She could bury herself in the jobs they were being paid to do and nothing else. Because everything else in her life was a hot mess.

It was almost seven-thirty in the evening and Del was still at the bar. He was sitting at one of the tables in the Bullpen area with his tablet and spiral notebooks spread out in front of him. He also had a beer that he'd only half finished and his cell phone within arm's reach.

"Read over the last financial statements you sent out this morning," Jeret, the former Texas Ranger said after taking a seat across from Del.

"We're pretty damn close to working in the black. Not many businesses can say that after only eighteen months," Jeret continued.

Del nodded without looking up from what he was doing.

"Yeah. I was pretty encouraged by the numbers after I ran them three times," he replied.

"You know Noah's claiming full credit because of his awesome marketing skills," Jeret said.

Del did look up then, and he frowned. "Of course, he is."

Jeret laughed, an infectious sound that Del knew he'd never forget. Jeret's Game Changers t-shirt was a couple sizes too small, which was exactly the way the guy liked it. This combined with his fitted jeans and chiseled good looks kept the women swarming the bar waiting for the opportunity to see him come out of the kitchen. And Jeret with his dark brown hair and hazel eyes loved every minute of the attention.

"He gave you a little credit for handling the social media thing," Jeret added.

Del shrugged. "It's not as bad as I thought it'd be."

If only they knew. While logging onto the social media app and posting about the bar since finding out who Mercedes-Girl926 was had felt a little different, he'd continued to do so, seeing growth in how many people replied to or simply liked the posts. Also, after figuring out how to go live on the app and starting a Karaoke Check-In on Wednesday nights, traffic in the bar on those nights as well as online interaction had increased. So yeah, it was working.

"This is working out a lot better than I thought too," Jeret said. "You know I had my reservations."

After mistakenly taking the life of an eight-year old boy who'd come out of nowhere when Jeret and his team were engaging a suspect, the military trained officer, turned chef, now had reservations about a lot of things. Del could relate to being cautious as well, his time at the DEA and the scandal that precipitated his early retirement was a prime example.

"Our plan was to come back and make a statement," Del said, trying to be as positive as possible. "We're doing that. Especially with our sponsorship of the youth little league and cheerleading teams and now Ethan's idea for the new youth center."

"Speaking of which, wedding plans are in full swing. We've gotta get the bachelor party together. Ethan's adamant about no strippers, which is fine, but we still need to come up with a fantastic going away celebration."

Del shook his head. "He's not going anywhere."

"Yeah, he is, going off to married life. The land where none of us have gone before," Jeret continued with a chuckle.

Jeret was right. None of them had ever talked about getting married. Their conversations about girls and then women had covered only the basic topics, dates and break-ups. Nothing about long term commitment, ever.

Del closed the book he'd been using to copy notes onto his electronic file and logged out of his tablet. "He seems pretty happy about it."

Jeret sat back in the chair and folded his arms across his chest. "Portia's a good woman. I don't think any of us saw that in her when we were in school."

Del agreed about Portia. "We weren't looking for it back then." He contemplated how true that statement was especially since he knew he'd never looked at Rylan the way he was now.

Jeret ran a hand over the stubble at his chin. "Yeah, we weren't looking for a lot of things back then. Anyway, we've rented a room at the resort for the actual party and a few guest rooms for afterwards because I'm pretty sure none of us will be in any shape to drive home."

"Sounds like a smart plan." A plan Del was glad he wasn't in charge of. He was about to say something else when his phone vibrated on the table. His frown was immediate the moment he recognized the number.

"Do me a favor and take this stuff back to the office for me. I'm gonna take this call outside," he said to Jeret.

"It's like twenty-five degrees outside and the temps are supposed to dip even lower as the night goes on," Jeret stated, confusion clear in his tone.

Del had already stood and picked up the still ringing phone. "I'm not gonna freeze to death taking a five-minute telephone call. But if I do, all my shares in the bar go to Camy." He walked away heading to one of the side doors.

Cursing came next as he stepped outside because it was rather brisk as the sun that had been high in the sky earlier—offering very little warmth—had long since set and now the indigo sky gave way to the cold. So, he stuffed one hand in the front pocket of his pants and answered the phone before it stopped ringing.

"Hey Del, it's Clark."

The familiar voice didn't make him feel any better about this call. "Hey Clark. What's up?"

"Sorry to call after normal business hours but I just wanted to give you a head's up that trial's starting next week in the Wimbley case."

Del's fingers clenched the phone. Renaldo Wimbley was a drug kingpin who was the subject of his last case while he was with the DEA.

"Okay," Del answered recalling the subpoena he'd stuck in his desk drawer at home. He'd wanted this case and that chapter in his life out of sight and out of mind for as long as possible. Apparently, that wasn't long enough.

"I know I can't tell you what to say when you take the stand, but I wanted to remind you that—"

"No." He snapped, cutting Clark off and shook his head before realizing the guy couldn't see him. "You don't have to remind me. I know what to say and more importantly what not to say." In the end, everything had rested on what Del hadn't said or done, including a woman's life.

"It's a delicate situation, Del," Clark continued.

"I know," he replied even though he still didn't totally understand what had happened. All he knew for certain was that he'd been the only one from the team to resign from the Agency. The only one who saw a problem with how things had played out the night of the raid on The Xstasy Club.

And probably the only one who felt guilty about Shannen Cranston's death.

"Look, I've got my own attorney and we've gone over the testimony I'm going to give. So, you don't have to worry."

"I wasn't worried." Clark lied.

Special Agent Clark Jones was deathly afraid of what Del could say, because in one sentence, Del could end Clark's illustrious career with the DEA and take a few politicians and other law enforcement agents down with him. But Del had no intention of doing that. Not now because all of that stuff was behind him.

"I just wanted you to know it was coming up, so you'll be prepared to face Wimbley again."

"I'm not afraid of him," Del said. "I never was." Which was all the more reason why testifying in this case was probably a very bad idea. Wimbley wasn't the forgiving type, nor was he the type to ever forget a face.

Clark cleared his throat. A sign that he didn't like what Del had just said. Del didn't give a damn. He didn't work for Clark anymore and he definitely didn't need the guy's approval of what he thought or said.

"So, thanks for the heads up. Guess I'll see you next week." There was no need in prolonging the call and besides that, Del had nothing but contempt for Clark and all the others that were wore the badge but acted like him.

"Yeah, see you next week," Clark replied and the call was disconnected.

Del pressed the button to clear the call from the screen and the call log on his phone. He stuck the phone in his back pocket and yanked open the door to the bar. Stepping back inside to the heat and the noise, he tried to find his center once again. Breathing in deeply, out slowly, he let the combined sounds of the televisions, music and guests chatting remind him of who and where he was now. He was a business owner, not a DEA agent. His job was to help run this bar and restaurant, not take down national drug lords or protect confidential informants.

But he couldn't help but remember the time when that was

his job and he'd failed dismally. Flexing his fingers at his side, he started moving, cutting through the tables of people and heading past the bar. He pushed through the kitchen doors and walked by the shelves of pots and pans and supplies, the two large sub-zero freezers and a host of sous chefs and waitstaff, to another door. This one led to staff bathrooms, the storeroom and two offices that the guys all shared. Del went into one of those offices and slammed the door closed behind him. He paced back and forth across the ten by ten space, trying to tamp down on his temper as the memories came crashing back, and with them the guilt and disappointment. Not that he'd felt, but as Del had always thought his mother would've felt if she'd lived to see what he'd done.

"Hey, you alright?" Lance asked the moment he opened the door and stepped inside.

When Del only stopped pacing and looked up at him, Lance closed the door.

"What happened? Jeret said you took a call outside. Who was it?"

He almost didn't answer Lance's question. Talking about his problems wasn't something Del subscribed to. But Lance wasn't just his twin—making them even closer and more in tune with each other than anyone else in the world—he'd also worked in law enforcement as a homicide detective at the Metropolitan Police Department. Which meant Lance was just as good as Del, if not better, at knowing when someone was lying.

"My old supervisor. He wanted to give me a heads up about the trial next week."

Lance knew the whole story. He was the only one Del had told every sordid detail to. The other brothers knew the reasons behind Del's resignation, they just didn't know the background emotional stuff. Some things only a twin could know.

Lance came over and sat on the side of the desk. He hated the chairs in the offices because he said they weren't built for men over six feet tall.

"Did you tell him to jerk off?" Lance asked snidely.

Del shook his head. "I should have."

"Look, you knew the trial was coming up and you know what you have to do. Just do it and get it over with. Don't let that asshole try to persuade you to do things his way. You don't work for him anymore."

"I didn't do things his way when I worked for him," Del said. "And look what happened as a result."

Lance shook his head. "That investigation was bound to go bad, man. We both know that."

Del stopped pacing. He dragged his hands down his face and took a deep breath before letting it out slowly.

"Yeah. You're right," he said. "Listen, I'm just gonna head home. I'll call Andy and let him know that Clark called me and then I'm not thinking about this mess anymore until I absolutely have to."

Which in Del's mind meant the moments before he walked onto the witness stand. He was through giving up parts of his life to a system that had given him nothing in return. Not when he was a teenager and accused of vandalism—the original cause for him ending up at the Grace House for Boys—and then again when he'd graduated from college despite his haters doubting he ever would.

"You did your job, Del. Don't let them make you doubt that," Lance insisted.

Del nodded as he approached the door. "I know. I did my job and I stood up for what I thought was right. I can live with those facts. Thanks, man," he said before opening the door and heading out to the bar so he could go home.

Lance didn't say anything in return. There was nothing else to be said. They were always there when the other needed them. Del hadn't told anyone about the phone call, but Lance had known something was wrong and had come to assist. For all the times he'd done that, Del would love his brother eternally. He just wished that none of the things that had happened to him and Lance while they lived in D.C. had ever happened. But the reality was that if those things hadn't happened in their lives, neither of them would be here in Providence now, running this bar with their friends.

And Del wouldn't be sleeping with Rylan. He couldn't explain why that was also a plus to being back in Providence, or why he took his phone out of his pocket as he climbed behind the wheel of the second SUV he'd rented, and sent her a text inviting her to his place for dinner tonight. Nothing involving the two of them made sense but being with her made Del feel good. He hadn't felt that way in far too long and he wasn't yet ready to give it up.

10

"This will be so much better than grilled cheese. Did you smell that onion gravy?" Rylan asked as she and Del walked out of Margie's carrying their bags full of the dinner Margie had prepared for them.

They were almost to their cars when Rylan heard her name being called. She turned so fast, thinking instantly that someone was seeing her and Del together. Camy already knew about them, that didn't mean Rylan wanted to risk anyone else finding out. She also didn't want Del to be angry that someone was seeing them together.

"Hey!" Naomi said as she fast walked across the parking lot. "Mom's been calling you. We need to schedule a date and time to go look at dresses and to think about Christmas dinner. Aunt Belle is bringing her new boyfriend and he has four kids."

"I'm spending Christmas with Dad and Uncle Larry." Rylan had planned to tell her mother and Naomi this in the next few days, but that announcement certainly wasn't planned to take place in the parking lot at Margie's.

Now, she moved until she stood directly in front of Naomi,

hoping to block Del from Naomi's view. Her sister never could focus on more than one thing at a time, and the one thing Naomi loved to focus on was herself.

"What? Why? Neither of them can cook. And you barely cook without Mom's help, so what do you plan to eat Ramen noodles?" Naomi asked, her tone tinged with sarcasm.

Naomi wore a houndstooth coat with black leather gloves. Her hair was neatly curled this time, her make-up light and natural. Rylan gripped the bag she was holding in her hand and tried not to feel like a bum wearing her work boots, jeans and sweatshirt beneath a coat that looked as if she were ready for the next snowball fight. Normally these things didn't bother her— okay, well they did a little—but now that she was with Del, she sort of wondered if he thought about women who dressed and looked like Naomi as more his style.

"He's our father," Rylan said. "I don't want to take sides and you shouldn't either."

"He's a thief," Naomi snapped.

Rylan was just about to respond when Del touched her arm. She hadn't realized he'd come up from behind to stand next to her. She also hadn't told him to go on to the truck to wait for her while she talked to her sister. So, looking over to see him standing close with a smile already in place shouldn't have been a surprise.

"Hi Naomi," he said. "It's been a while since I've seen you."

"Oh. Del. Hello," Naomi said and looked from him to Rylan and then back to Del. "What're you doing here? Did you just come from Margie's too? Thursday's smothered pork chops and onion gray. It's the only night that I bother to eat any kind of take out."

"It's the night Mom works late at the school so she's not home to cook dinner," Rylan corrected her sister.

Naomi shot her a quick, heated glance.

"Anyway, I haven't seen you in a while either," Naomi said to Del.

She'd already switched from the slightly irritated look she'd been given Rylan to the sweet and sultry look she was now giving Del.

"I heard you and your little friends opened a bar. I just haven't had time to get over there," she was saying.

Del just nodded. "It's okay, we plan on sticking around for a while."

"Oh, I know! Do you book private parties?" Naomi asked, her brown eyes now alight with glee.

"Yeah we do. We have an upper level called The Skybox especially for private parties. You havin' a party?" Del asked.

Naomi nodded and with one hand snatched the glove off her other. She thrust the left hand into Del's face so fast it was a wonder he didn't get scratched by her long pink-painted nails.

"I'm engaged!" Naomi said and did a little happy dance right there in the parking lot.

Rylan rolled her eyes, but she'd turned her head so that nobody would see that's what she was doing. Her mother had sent her text two days ago announcing Naomi's great news. Rylan had, in return, sent her sister the obligatory congratulations. It wasn't that she wasn't happy for Naomi, she was. Her sister deserved happiness just like everybody else, even if Naomi wasn't good at making people feel particularly happy herself. But the tone of her mother's message had implied that once again, Naomi was doing so much better than Rylan.

"Really? That's fantastic! Congratulations!" Del told her. "We'd love to host your engagement party. Just stop by the bar in the next couple of days and we'll give you a tour of the Skybox and you can confirm your booking."

"I'll have to see when Ellis's next game is," Naomi said. "But thinking about it now, it's really perfect. Announcing our engagement at a sports bar is genius. Ellis is going to love it and his teammates can come and any of those other players he wants to invite. What's the capacity in this Skybox area? We may need to rent out the entire place."

For a moment Del looked confused.

Rylan, irritated that they were standing in the very public parking lot while her food was getting cold, decided to help him out.

"Naomi is engaged to Ellis Colby, the top scoring point guard in the NBA this season." She could've seemed a little more enthusiastic about that especially since she enjoyed basketball, but Naomi was working her nerves with this impromptu interruption.

The quick and lethal glare Naomi cut her seconds after she finished meant her sister wasn't pleased with her at the moment either.

"Damn, Ellis Colby? Well, hell yeah, we'll rent the whole place out to you for the engagement party. I'd have to go over some things logistically with the guys but we can definitely make this happen," Del said, excitement clear in his tone.

Rylan felt guilty at that point. Why hadn't she thought about suggesting the engagement party be at the bar? Naomi was right, it was a genius idea. That didn't mean she cared anymore about this wedding than she had ten minutes ago.

"Okay, I'm going to go right home after I get my pork chops and call my event planner. We're going to start working on this ASAP. Do you have a card or something?" Naomi asked.

"The bar is a ten-minute drive from the house, Naomi. You can drive over and speak to Del and the guys just like he suggested," Rylan said. "And why don't you plan to do that tomorrow or the next day. Whenever. I'd like to eat my food before it gets cold."

Naomi looked unbothered. "Well, you can run along. Del and I are discussing business."

When Rylan hesitated, Del stepped in. "It'll be better if you come down to the bar, Naomi. That way you can get a look around and make sure it's what you want. Talk to your planner and then we can schedule a time for the tour."

"Sure," Naomi said. "But you really should get some cards, Del. If you guys are running a business, you need to run it correctly."

"Yeah, thanks," Del told her. "I'll get right on that."

"Goodnight, Naomi," Rylan said and went to her car.

Del moved when she did, walking her to the door of her car and waiting while she got in. "I'll be right behind you," he said as he leaned down and kissed her lightly on the lips.

The act shocked the cold out of Rylan and she sat there blinking at him for endless seconds. She knew that Naomi was still standing there because she'd heard her sister gasp. And since she wasn't sure what to say to Del at the moment and definitely didn't want to hear anymore of Naomi's comments, Rylan closed the door and started the engine.

Rylan thought she'd lost her appetite, but once she was inside Del's house and he told her to have a seat while he heated the food and fixed their drinks, she realized she was still hungry.

And she was still annoyed. Not so much at Naomi anymore, because her sister was just being her usual self-absorbed self. Even when she'd texted Rylan asking if she could get a discount on renting out the bar since Rylan was obviously sleeping with Del. Rylan hadn't even bothered to respond. She had considered how Del was going to feel about someone else in town knowing about their little fling. Secrets never stayed secrets for long in Providence.

She was walking around the large living room admiring the modern décor mixed with pieces that she knew had come from his mother's house when it dawned on her that Del had actually kissed her. Right in front of Naomi, as if he didn't give a damn who saw them. The thought made her smile as she stood at the bay window looking out to the dark street.

"There are some TV trays over in that corner. Bring two over and we can eat here in front of the television."

She hadn't startled at Del's voice, but Rylan did turn to look at him first. He'd taken off the Game Changers shirt and now wore only a white t-shirt and jeans. Even that looked scrumptious on him. Or was she just thinking about food?

"What?" Del asked.

When she realized she was still standing in the same spot while he was holding two plates of steaming food, she shrugged. "Ah, I was thinking that this is a great spot for a Christmas tree. When do you normally put yours up?"

She could've just asked him about that kiss. Why he'd done it? What it meant that he'd done it in front of her sister, or anyone else who'd could've been walking by? But she didn't, instead, she moved to the other side of the room, past a curio cabinet that held over fifty bells inside. She recalled his mother had collected bells. There'd been three shelves full of them in the house where Camy now lived. Obviously, the siblings had divided them so they could all have something of their mother's.

"I wasn't going to put up a tree," he said once she had the trays set up and he'd put down the plates. "I'll get the drinks. Find something on television."

Rylan found the television remote on the glass table beside the light gray couch. That was a good place for them. Instead of between the cushions on the couch, or under the pillows in her bed. She turned on the sixty-five-inch flat screen that was mounted above the natural fireplace. When she found a holiday favorite, she set the remote back on the table and sat down. Del came in with glasses of iced tea and groaned.

"I thought you weren't into those holiday movies like Camy," he complained as he sat.

"This is a classic, just like *Christmas Vacation*. I usually watch it at least once a season, if not more," she said.

"It's ridiculous," Del said. "Who gets on a plane and leaves their kid at home? Even though she has a bunch of kids, it's still a little far-fetched. And then to make a sequel where the parents do the same thing, but this time the kid ends up in another state. Unreal."

"Um hmmm," she nodded and gazed at him.

"Um hmmm, what?"

"You've watched this series more than once, haven't you?" she asked narrowing her eyes at him.

"I lived with Camy," he replied.

Rylan chuckled. "Enough said."

They ate in companionable silence for a few minutes, until Kevin's parents realized they overslept and the entire house full of people begin to get ready to leave for the airport.

"How come Kevin didn't hear all that hoopla?" Del asked before forking another scoop of mashed potatoes into his mouth.

"He's a heavy sleeper," she replied and listened to Del laugh. "It's not funny. I've always been a heavy sleeper, which is why Naomi always got downstairs to open her gifts on Christmas morning before me."

Del shook his head. "My mom made us all wait to go down at the same time. Lance used to take forever in the bathroom washing his face and brushing his teeth. Camy would whine and lay on her stomach at the top of the stairs to see if she could see anything down in the living room."

Rylan smiled at the thought. Things had always been different at the Greer house. That was one of the reasons she'd always wanted to stay there.

"Camy's still like that, you know. Two years ago, we went to a ski resort for the holidays. You and Lance weren't able to come home and she was feeling really sad that she'd be alone. Because my family's a little more dysfunctional, I had no problem scheduling a trip for us. We partied on Christmas Eve and drank so much I thought I was on another planet." Rylan laughed at the memory. "But early the next morning, even before the sun rose, Camy was in my room, jumping on the bed telling me to get up so we could exchange our gifts. I was like, girl you are outta your mind. But she was dead serious."

Del continued to laugh. "Yeah, that sounds just like her. Camy's always loved Christmas. So did my mom."

"And that's why you and Lance can take it or leave it," she said and watched Del put down his fork and sit back on the couch.

"I'm sorry if that's too personal," she told him. "You don't have to talk about it if you don't want to."

He waited a beat before shrugging. "Not talking about it doesn't make it better."

Rylan chewed the food she'd just put into her mouth slowly.

"My mom loved Christmas. She loved all of us being happy together. After my dad died, a big chunk of that happiness went with him. Lance and I didn't handle that very well," Del said somberly.

"You got into some sort of trouble each time you left the house," Rylan said then clapped her mouth shut.

He nodded. "That's accurate."

"But that last time, when the principal wanted to press charges against us and Mal's dad was all for the idea of sending fifteen-year olds to jail, it was just too much for my mom. At first,

Lance and I were pretty pissed off that she sent us to The House, but then we realized we probably deserved it. We were hellions and it wasn't fair when my mom was trying to do everything by herself. Then I broke Mal's nose a few months before I was supposed to come back home and they decided to add more time to my stay at the House instead of sending me to juvie." He shook his head, a mixture of shame and sorrow marring his face. "I hated that I kept disappointing my mother so much."

"She was proud that you graduated from high school and then went off to college," Rylan told him because she'd been there to see his mother smiling gleefully when she found out her son was going to be a college graduate.

"More like relieved," Del said.

Rylan shook her head. "No, Del. She was definitely proud. I remember hearing her tell Mr. Penning one Sunday after church that her boys were going to do great things. That they were independent and smart and confident. Of course, she was taking jabs at Mal who still hadn't decided if he was going to college or staying here to work in the office with his dad."

"Which he did."

"He did. Because he was too chickenshit to try anything else," she replied.

Del laughed. "You never were one to mince words."

Rylan shook her head. "No, I wasn't. Which is why I'm going to tell you that we need to get you a Christmas tree, put it right in front of that window and then get out there and decorate that great front yard you have."

For a minute he looked as if he were going to say no, but then he smiled. "Yeah, that sounds like a good idea."

He leaned across the couch and took her hand. "You were a good idea," he said softly.

"I was a mistake, remember," she replied when an unexpected pang registered in her chest.

Del shook his head. "Nah. My mom always said that things happened for a reason."

He was rubbing her hand, threading his fingers between hers and Rylan was thoroughly enjoying the feel and the look of their entwined fingers. She was enjoying sitting here after work having dinner in front of the television with Del. More than she'd ever enjoyed anything else before.

When he lifted her hand to his lips and kissed each one of her fingers, that pang in her chest shifted to what felt like her heart plummeting full speed to the pit of her stomach. Oh no.

"Come here," he whispered.

She hesitated, or at least in her mind she did. Her body, on the other hand had already begun leaning over until her face was aligned with his.

"Make no mistake that this is intentional," he said quietly. "Everything from this moment on is exactly what I want. Understand?"

Rylan nodded. "I understand."

The word had barely slipped from her lips when Del's touched hers in a whisper-soft kiss that sent warm tendrils soaring through her body. With his free hand, he touched her cheek as the kiss went from a soft touch to a thorough exploration. Then his hand was in her hair, his blunt-tipped fingers scraping along her scalp as he held her face close to his. Rylan made the next move. She broke the kiss just long enough to move across the couch, pushing Del up to a sitting position before straddling him.

"From this point on, everything I do is intentional," she said, tossing his words back at him.

He grinned. "I'm definitely down for that."

"I'll remember you said that," she whispered and laced her arms around his neck.

She nuzzled her center right up against his awakening dick, not giving a damn that they were both still fully clothed, just wanting the contact anyway she could get it at the moment and traced her tongue over his lips. Del moved his hands up her back and then down to cup her ass and press her even closer to his length. She sucked his tongue into her mouth and loved the sound of him groaning in response. He grabbed the hem of her sweatshirt and forced her to break contact so he could lift it up over her head. His palms immediately cupped her breasts through the fitted t-shirt she wore beneath and she arched her back to give him unfettered access.

"You have great hands," she told him.

"You have great breasts," he replied.

She chuckled and moved in for another kiss. Their tongues dueled like long lost friends and her fingers gripped his shoulders. She was so ready to rip all his clothes off and ride him on this couch until they both exploded with pleasure. But a beeping sound, followed by a door opening and an unmistakable, "Oh shit!" interrupted them.

$\mathcal{D}$el returned to the living room after walking Rylan upstairs to his bedroom and leaving her there. The television was still on. The trays with their empty plates of food and glasses still sitting in front of the couch. Lance stood by the window staring out into the evening.

"Guess I should give your key back," Lance said when he turned to face Del.

Del picked up the remote and turned the television off.

"I'm not usually in my living room about to have sex with a woman," he snapped before moving to the tables and gathering the places and glasses.

He heard Lance folding the tables as he walked into the kitchen. A few seconds later, Lance was in the kitchen too.

"So, you and Rylan, huh?"

Del closed the dishwasher after putting the dishes inside.

"Is that a problem for you?"

Lance shrugged. "Nah, not me. But what about Camy?"

Del didn't pretend he hadn't thought about how his sister would feel about him sleeping with her best friend. But truthfully, he hadn't given it a whole lot of consideration either. He and Rylan were adults, they could do whatever they wanted.

"It's not that big of a deal," he said but noted how hollow and dishonest the words sounded to his ears.

"You said the same thing about Shannen," Lance said.

Del shook his head. "Don't do that!"

Lance didn't flinch at his brother's raised voice.

"You don't know anything," Del said. "You always think you do, but you don't. First, you want to tell me how I should feel about how things went down in D.C. and what I should and shouldn't feel guilty about. And now, you're here talking about who I should and shouldn't sleep with. There's no comparison to Shannen. None. At. All."

When he was finished Del had headed out of the kitchen, but he stopped when only silence followed.

"Shannen should've never happened." Those very true and still awkwardly painful words came quietly. He didn't turn back to Lance because he didn't want to look into a face similar to his own and talk about the worst time in his life. Not again. "And this thing with Rylan, it wasn't supposed to happen either. But I feel like this is different, man. I can't explain it, but it just is."

"Then go for it," Lance told him. "If it feels like something you should pursue, then do it. But don't lie to yourself in the process. That's not going to end well for either of you."

Lance pushed past Del at that moment.

As he walked away, he told his brother, "I'll ring the bell first from now on."

Del didn't respond. He knew that Lance was right. He also knew that there wasn't much he could do about it. After locking up the house, Del headed upstairs. He wasn't sure what Rylan's reaction to what had just happened was going to be, but he knew that he would have to address it. Today had been a hell of a day, and each time he'd thought things were getting a little brighter a big fat monkey wrench was tossed into his plan.

She was sitting in his recliner, one leg crossed over the other, flipping pages in one of his photo albums. And she looked as if she lived there. Like they shared this room and this was part of her normal evening routine. He shook his head at how surprisingly good that thought made him feel and walked further into the room.

"Sorry about that," he murmured and sat on the edge of his bed. "We all have keys to each other's houses."

Rylan let her hand rest on the album and nodded. "I know. Camy insists that she always knocks or rings the doorbell first because her eyes wouldn't be able to stand what she might see if she didn't." Ryland laughed. "I'm almost glad it was Lance that decided to stop by instead of her or you might be responsible for blinding your sister."

He was glad she could laugh about this. Come to think of it, he never really recalled seeing Rylan overly upset about anything. She had a very relaxed and confident personality, one that Del knew for certain had rubbed off on Camy. Well, at least the confident part had. Camy could still go off like a firecracker at any given moment. He wondered how she would react if he told her everything.

"Well, Lance is cool with this. I mean, his eyes certainly aren't going to suffer. He's seen far worse than what he walked in on," Del told her.

"I'm sure both of you have in the line of work you used to be in. Look, Del, I know we didn't plan for this...ah, this...thing between us. And I can totally understand if your intention was to keep it under wraps."

"Stop," he told her and held up a hand just in case she didn't follow his word. "No, we didn't plan for this. But I'm absolutely not embarrassed by it."

He took a deep breath and let it out slowly.

"Before I left the DEA, I was involved with a woman," he started.

Rylan sat back in the chair and closed the photo album slowly.

"She was a confidential informant, so I should've steered clear from her, but I didn't. I also didn't tell anyone I was seeing her. Not just because I could've lost my job, but because I felt uncomfortable being with a person who sold drugs, especially in my situation. But when I learned that she was selling drugs to pay for the nursing home where her mom lived, I thought differently of her." He ran his hands down his face. "Anyway, things went south on a raid and she was killed. I blamed myself for not being able to protect her and for not being more sensitive to what she may've needed out of our relationship.

"That's not what I'm doing here, Rylan. You're right, we haven't discussed what this is between us and I guess we should at some point. But I really need you to know that I could never be embarrassed by you." He meant those words with everything that he was.

She sighed heavily. "That's good to hear."

Her words may have sounded nice, but he didn't like how she looked when she'd said them. "Are you sure?"

"Yes," she told him. "You have no idea how hard it is growing up in the shadow of a beauty pageant winning sister and a gorgeous and vivacious best friend. Sometimes I feel like I get lost between the two of them. But as I grew older, I realized that wasn't really the case. Everybody has their own cross to bear and light to shine. Mine is in the auto mechanic business, that's why I'm fighting so hard to keep my dad's shop."

Del could only stare at her for a few seconds. The woman that she'd grown into amazed him.

"Your dad's losing the auto shop? I can't imagine that place not being there," he said. Up until a few days ago he may not have visited it much, but Kent Automotive was a landmark fixture on the corner of Maple and Valley Roads.

"Me either. Between there and your mom's house, I don't know which place I stayed at most as a child. But he and my mom are divorcing and, in the drama-filled back and forth that comes from a decades' old relationship, the body shop has become the bone that each want to claim."

He was a bit confused by the logic of that scenario. "Your mother never struck me as the body shop type."

"Oh, she's not," Rylan continued. "She's the money type. Her and Naomi, hence Naomi's NBA player fiancé."

Del nodded. He could definitely see that in Naomi's personality, which is why none of the guys he knew had ever thought about asking her out. Naomi Kent had made it perfectly clear from around the time that she was thirteen years old that there would never be a guy in Providence that was good enough for her. Rylan was nothing like her sister or her mother, for that matter. She was unique.

"I guess we've both got baggage and are damaged in our own ways," he said and stood. "There's only one solution for that."

He held out a hand to her. She looked at that hand and then pushed the photo album off her lap to rest in the side of the chair before she put her hand in his and stood.

"What's the solution?"

"We do whatever it takes to make each other feel good, for as long as we possibly can," he said bringing her hand up to kiss each one of her fingers.

She tilted her head, until her ponytail did this flopping thing that was together child-like and alluring.

"I think I can co-sign that," she said and stepped closer until he wrapped his arms around her waist.

She could co-sign and she could ride.

It had only taken a few minutes for both of them to get naked and less time than that for Rylan to sit on the edge of the bed and take his heavy length between her hands. Del's whole body tensed. He could do nothing but stare down at her as he held the condom packet in his hand. She was looking at his dick as if it had been part of the meal they'd purchased from Margie's and he swore he'd never seen anything sexier.

"Put it on," he told her, practically thrusting the condom in front of her face.

He was afraid that with her holding him the way she was and staring at him the way she did, that he would come in her hand at any second totally embarrassing himself.

But she shook her head.

"Not yet."

She licked her lips and parted them, leaning forward to touch them to the tip of his dick before Del could even blink.

"Fuck!" He moaned as pleasure shot through his body like lightening with the touch of her tongue. Her mouth was so freakin' hot, her slim fingers so damn strong as she gripped him at the base and stroked upward while her mouth covered him. She moved fast, as if she thought he might stop her before she could finish. It was a fleeting thought in Del's mind, but he was afraid he might actually be paralyzed at the moment. He watched as her cheeks hollowed and she took long drags on his dick. She bobbed her head, one hand moving to his heavy sac, kneading until he could see starbursts behind his closed eyes.

His hands went to her hair, fingers pushed with pressure until that infernal ban slipped off and her hair was finally freed. Del raked his fingers over her scalp, gripping her soft hair in his fingers and hold tight as he started to pump with the ministrations of her mouth. His breathing was frantic as her mouth made a loud sucking sound over his rigid length. He pumped faster, she sucked harder. He was going to come. She wasn't stopping. He couldn't do it. Not to Rylan. But damn, how he wanted to. And if she didn't get her mouth off him, he certainly was going to blow.

With all the strength he possessed at the moment, he pushed Rylan's head away and stepped back.

"Put. It. On. Now," he said through clenched teeth without chancing another look down at her.

He knew her lips would be swollen and wet, just as his dick was still rock hard and probably glistening from her mouth. He needed to get inside her as soon as possible. Relief flashed through him as he heard her tearing the condom packet and felt her fingers on him once more, this time sheathing him. Del was about to push her back on the bed, but Rylan moved fast. She stood, wrapping her arms around his neck and then turned them both until Del fell back on the bed and she landed on top of him.

"Tricky." He grinned while looking up into her warm brown eyes.

She licked her lips. "You have no idea."

And with that she straddled him, reaching between their bodies to grab his dick and guide him inside of her. When she sat atop him, acclimating to his depth, Del thought he'd died and gone to heaven. She looked like an African goddess sitting atop him with her gold and black hair and heavenly body. Then she began to move. Slow, tortuous movements at first before picking up her pace.

Del grasped her hips, holding on tightly as he lifted up from the bed to meet her pumps with his thrusts. They were loud, her screams, his moans, the slapping of their bodies. Loud and boisterous and the best he'd ever had.

Her legs trembled first and Del watched as her release claimed her.

"Beautiful," he whispered knowing he'd never seen anything like Rylan before.

She collapsed over him and Del wrapped her in his arms. He

rolled them over and began moving slowly in and out of her. She'd wrapped her legs around his waist and buried her face in his neck, her blunt-tipped nails pressing into his back. He moved methodically, loving the smooth and easy stroking and the undeniable build of desire trailing up his spine.

Had it ever been like this before?

No. Not even with Shannen.

But this wasn't Shannen. There were no secrets between him and Rylan. They'd known each other too long for that. She was with him because she wanted to be, not because she needed him to save her. Hell, after tonight, Del felt like Rylan might actually be saving him.

He didn't know what to do with that thought so he pumped faster, lost himself in her heated flesh and the tight suction of her muscles contracting once again around his length. He groaned, hugging her so tight to him he feared he might cause physical damage. His release exploded from him, jerking his mind and his thoughts until he was confused and blinded by any coherent thought. All he could think about was Rylan and how she'd changed everything he'd thought he was supposed to be doing with his life at this moment.

All he could think about was staying safely inside of her, enjoying her...loving... Del pulled back at that second. He looked down into her passion-riddled gaze and couldn't figure out what to say. And because there were no words, he simply kissed her.

"You know we need to get a life when all we can think of to do on a Friday night is to go the bar where we know every guy that's going to be there and none of them are prospects," Camy said.

Rylan didn't respond but pulled into the parking lot and cut the engine.

"Oh, I forgot, you've already got a guy to go home to," Camy continued before reaching over to pinch Rylan's arm.

"Ow! What did I do?" Rylan whined.

"You're getting laid on the regular and I'm forced to keep batteries on hand for Mr. Morris and me to share our love," she said and climbed out of the car.

Rylan got out and slammed the door. Mr. Morris was what Camy had named her high-powered vibrator. It was after her movie-star crush Morris Chestnut and quite frankly was keeping Camy company for a few months before Rylan and Del hooked up. But Rylan wasn't going to remind her of that fact.

"And besides, it hasn't been really on a regular. We've had a few new vehicles down at the shop so the last few days I've been working pretty late. And Del's been on the night shift at the bar and by the time he gets off I'm already asleep so he doesn't come over and—"

"You can stop now," Camy said. "Just because I'm cool with you bumping uglies with my brother, doesn't mean I want to hear the gory details."

Rylan grinned because she hadn't begun to give Camy details about her and Del's amazing sex life. Instead, she held the door to the bar open and smiled sweetly at Camy as she said, "You used to always beg for details."

Camy made a yuck face and walked into the bar leaving Rylan standing out in the cold.

Chuckling, Rylan headed in behind her. They eased through the Friday night crowd, making their way to two vacant seats all the way at the end of the bar. Rylan removed her coat and crossed her purse over her chest. Camy had been texting her all day trying to figure out what they were going to do tonight. When they finally settled on coming to the bar for drinks and nachos, Rylan left work and raced home to change. No way was she showing up at the bar—where she knew Del was going to be —dressed in dirty old jeans and an even dirtier sweatshirt because everything from oil to antifreeze had spilled on her today.

The bar was really jumping tonight. All of the television sets were going, Ethan and Lance were behind the bar taking care of drink orders, there was a group in the Bullpen and the rope had been removed from the steps, so there was an event going on upstairs as well. The crowd made her smile because that meant Del and his brothers were doing good business. Rylan knew this place was important to them and she couldn't help but feel a swell of pride at knowing the great guys who'd brought this idea to life.

"Hey Slick!" Rock said coming up behind her, clapping a hand on her shoulder.

Rylan leaned into his light embrace. "Hey yourself. Things are looking good in here."

"Yeah, but then you two came in," he joked.

Camy gave him the finger and continued to study the menu.

"She loves me," Rock told Rylan.

Rylan wasn't so sure about that. Camy and Rock always did have a love/hate relationship.

"What's good on the grill tonight, Rock?" Rylan asked. "Jeret cooking up anything special?"

When the restaurant first opened, Jeret insisted that his experience only went as far as the four months he was a short order cook in Montana. As far as Rylan knew, nobody had ever figured out what Jeret was doing in Montana. And Jeret wasn't the type of guy a person just rattled off questions to. Not if that person expected to live.

"He's got some type of sausage wrap he's been bragging about. I've seen a few people ordering it and when I went back around to check on them, their plates were clean and they said it was good.

But I haven't tasted it myself. Trying to cut back on my meat intake," Rock told her.

He slipped his hand from her shoulder and rubbed it across his stomach. The ridiculously toned stomach. Rylan didn't laugh, but she did shake her head at his foolishness. There wasn't an ounce of fat on Rock's perfectly sculpted body. Only muscle on top of muscle.

"Well, we're not going the vegan route," Camy yelled over the music. "So, go on back and tell Jeret we'll have two of his sausage specials. And I'd like a beer."

Rock leaned in, pushing Rylan back so he could get closer to Camy.

"I'm not the waiter," he said.

Camy kissed the tip of his nose. "I know. You're the trouble-maker. But you're also the only one not busy so you can ease on back there and put our order in. What're you drinking, Rylan?"

"And don't say vodka," Rock warned as he slowly backed away from Camy.

Rylan recalled the night she'd been attempting to leave here in a drunken stupor, but Rock had put a halt to that with a glass of water and the announcement of GCSports18's identity. So much had changed in the few weeks since that time.

Rylan still rolled her eyes at him. "Fine. I'll have a glass of white wine. Is that better?"

"Much better," he said with a grin that was designed to make women swoon.

As for Rylan and Camy, they both groaned and waved him away.

"He's such a big oaf sometimes," Rylan complained.

"They all are," Camy countered. "Except that one, I guess."

Rylan watched the direction of Camy's gaze and tried her best not to blush when she locked gazes with Del.

"Great, now he thinks I've been sitting here staring at him the whole time," she snapped and looked away.

Camy laughed. "You've certainly been looking all around the place for him."

She resisted the urge to look in his direction again. "Have not."

"Girl, please. First, you know you can't lie to me and second, I've been sitting right here watching you."

"Well, it might help you find someone to take the place of Mr. Morris tonight if you'd look at someone other than me," Rylan quipped.

Something happened on the television and a group of guys cheered from across the room. Mariah Carey's *All I Want for Christmas Is You* came on and a chorus of women standing near the door began to sing their rendition of the holiday hit. A more cheerful setting Rylan couldn't have imagined if she'd tried. And for once in the past few months she felt relaxed enough to simply enjoy the atmosphere and not give a second thought to her family problems.

"Well excuse me if I'm basking in my best friend's glow of love." Camy continued their conversation.

That last word had Rylan tensing. "Oh no, Del and I are just…we're like really good friends with benefits or something like that," she told Camy.

The words didn't sound right to her ears, so Rylan wasn't at all surprised when Camy looked at her as if she were crazy and said, "Again, don't even try it."

They had both turned so that their backs faced the bar and they could participate in the people-watching pastime. Camy crossed one leg over the other, her thigh-high suede boots looking stylish and sexy at the same time. The shiny black leggings she wore beneath the boots shaped her thighs while a festive red sweater that molded to her every curve accentuated her D cup breasts.

As for Rylan, she'd chosen a cute black corduroy mini-skirt over gray sweater-tights and a long-sleeved gray bodysuit topped off with ankle boots that she'd had for two years but hardly ever wore. They probably looked as if they were trying to pick up men, which they sort of were.

"You know he's watching you too," Camy said with a grin.

Rylan didn't turn her head to look. Years of going to bars or clubs with Camy had taught her that. Never look at the subject at hand.

"It's his job to watch everyone in his establishment. He needs to make sure his customers are doing okay. He is the manager you know."

"Uh huh. Well, I think he's keeping an eye on his woman with all these available guys in the house tonight," Camy replied.

To prove her point about available guys, when one came up to Camy just seconds after her remark and asked if she'd like to dance, Rylan watched her friend smile and wink in her direction. There wasn't really much dancing space in Game Changers, but from time-to-time, people did have a tendency to get up and move to the rhythm of a favored song. Rylan remained seated, her elbows resting back on the bar as she continued people watching while waiting for their food.

"You trying to kill me or what?" Del asked when he came up to stand beside her.

He smelled terrific. Dolce and Gabbana's *The One*. She'd seen the bottle on his dresser along with a couple of others, but this was her favorite. He looked fabulous too wearing all black tonight from his Game Changers polo down to his black Timberland boots.

"Excuse me?" she asked. "I haven't seen or talked to you all day."

Del stood remarkably close to her without actually touching her and Rylan desperately wanted to loop her arms around his neck and touch her warm berry glossed lips to his. But there were way too many people in here for her to venture into the area of PDAs. While Del had made it clear that he had no problem being seen with her or people knowing that they were sort of together at the moment, Rylan still wanted to err on the side of caution.

"Then please let me apologize for that misstep. Because this punishment you're inflicting is torture."

He stepped in front of her at that moment, resting his palms on her knees. Heat soared up her legs and straight to her crotch leaving her speechless for a few seconds.

"Are those the kind of lines you're used to using on women?" she asked when she regained her senses.

Del was touching her quite intimately in the middle of his restaurant. Her heart was thumping wildly at the thought.

He shook his head, his sexy grin spreading.

"Just you," he told her and leaned forward to kiss first her cheek and then the spot beneath her ear.

Rylan couldn't help it; her hands came to Del's shoulders. Otherwise she was sure to fall off the stool.

"Oh please, can't you two get a room?" Lance said from behind her.

Rylan tilted her head back to see him delivering her and Camy's drinks.

"Hey Lance," she said.

Lance tapped Rylan's forehead the way he used to when they were young. "Hey Rylan. When you turn him loose tell him we've got orders in the back he can help bring out."

Before she could reply, Noah came up behind Del.

"Is this the type of establishment we're running here? You get to feel your woman up right here at the bar?" he asked.

Rylan did blush then because Del didn't move away from her

but shifted so that he was once again at her side, his arm draped over her shoulder. Of course, she was aware that Lance knew about her and Del, but since she'd been working late, she hadn't been into the bar or anywhere else that she would've seen the rest of the brothers. So, she didn't know they were in the loop about her and Del. However, she should've presumed they knew. Those six guys stuck together like glue, sharing every secret they had.

"Your marketing efforts are working like a charm," she said to Noah. "One of the cars I worked on yesterday had a flyer in the passenger seat."

Noah nodded, his dark hair slicked back from his face, goatee trimmed neatly and those dark eyes assessing everything in their path. Noah's father had been West Indian, moving here with Noah's grandfather when Noah was just three years old. Rylan and Camy had learned that Noah's mother, who Noah had no memory of, was a Caucasian woman who chose her career in medicine over a family in Providence, Virginia.

"Good to hear," he replied.

Del followed with a quick and instantly irritated, "Crap!"

Lance apparently seeing the same thing Del had, said, "Don't let him phase you. We can take his money just like we take everyone else's."

Rylan followed their gaze to see that Mal Penning dressed in jeans and a sport coat had just walked in.

"He's still the biggest idiot in town," Noah said after turning to see Mal.

"This is true," Rylan replied.

She reached out to take Del's hand, lacing her fingers with his. He lifted that hand and kissed her fingers.

"Fuck him," he whispered.

Rylan smiled because that was a much better reaction to Mal than the one Del had a few weeks ago at Margie's. She hadn't seen him that irritated in years, and truth be told, was in no hurry to see him that way again. So, operating on pure instinct, Rylan slipped off the stool, pulling Del along with her and said, "Let's dance."

He followed her a few feet away from his friends, but quickly said, "They're playing another Christmas song."

Rylan nodded because this one was a favorite of hers. Stevie Wonder's *Someday at Christmas.*

"It's fine. I love this one," Rylan told him and lifted her arms to drape over his shoulders.

Del laced his arms around her waist and they swayed to the festive tune. The fact that this was her favorite holiday song and she was in the arms of the strong, independent and compassionate man that made her feel like no one ever had before, was saying a lot.

It was saying something that Rylan wasn't sure she was ready to hear.

12

On Monday morning, Rylan walked into the auto shop feeling refreshed and well-loved...no, that wasn't the correct word. She'd spent the weekend at Del's place. On Saturday morning the two of them had gone to a Christmas tree farm and cut down the biggest Balsam Fir tree either of them had ever seen. They'd wrestled the tree on top of the SUV Del was still renting because the part for his truck had been delayed. And when they arrived at his place, had laughed and frolicked in the first snowflakes to fall in Providence while dragging the tree into his house.

Camy had divided all of their mother's Christmas decorations and brought Del's share over to his house later that afternoon. By evening, the guys were trying out a new manager and full staff at the bar that didn't include any of them. So Del's house was full of his friends, Camy, Portia, Rylan and hot chocolate laced this time with peppermint vodka. Rylan had never laughed so much as she did that day when they were decorating and absolutely murdering every Christmas song that was played through the speakers in Del's living room.

They had so much fun together, all of them, laughing and singing, reminiscing about happy times and planning for the future. Yes, there was a ski trip on tap for Valentine's Day, a bowling tournament in the spring because Jeret felt as though he was king of the pins, a Fourth of July BBQ and maybe a trip to Virginia Beach if the guys could all get away. Rylan found herself looking forward to everything, all while Del remained close to her throughout the day. There wasn't a moment that he wasn't reaching out to touch her hand or rub his fingers over her cheek. When they came around to the same side of the tree and attempted to hang an ornament on the same branch, he'd smiled and leaned in for a kiss.

And after everyone had left, Del had made slow, sweet passionate love to Rylan right there on the floor in front of the tree with its twinkling colorful lights.

Sunday morning, they'd slept in and when Del had gone to the bar later that afternoon, Portia, Rylan and Camy had gone to the outlets to do some Christmas shopping. So, this morning, even though it was the start of a new work week, Rylan was smiling and happier than she'd ever been because Del was in her life.

They were now a "thing" as Camy had pointed out yesterday.

"I don't care if the two of you refuse to give what you're doing a real title. It's a "thing" and you're both glowing while doing it. So there, be happy and move on," she'd snapped when Rylan had insisted she not call her and Del a couple.

It was true, Rylan and Del didn't give what they were doing a specific title. They just kept doing it. And with each time, each moment they spent together and each time they actually did "it", Rylan felt herself falling deeper and deeper.

She sighed when she walked into her office and removed her coat. Hanging it on the hook behind her door, she was on her way to her desk when her father came in.

"Good morning," Will said as he entered.

"Mornin, Daddy," Rylan replied and pulled out her chair to take a seat. "How's it going? Do we still have those two in the bay to work on?"

Will reached up and pulled the worn Baltimore Orioles hat he loved to wear from his head. He scratched a spot on his scalp and sat in one of the guest chairs across from Rylan's desk.

"Nope. I took care of them on Saturday while you were out," he said.

Rylan let her palms fall to her desk and sighed. "Daddy, you didn't have to do that. We decided that you would only stay open until noon and then you'd head home since I wasn't coming in."

Will shook his head. "Nothing to head home to," he said with a shrug.

His words sounded desolate, but true, and Rylan's heart hurt for him.

"Well, I'll work this Saturday and you take the day off. Maybe you and Uncle Larry can finally go get a tree and put up some decorations. Christmas is next Tuesday you know."

Which reminded Rylan she needed to get Uncle Larry and Aunt Belle gifts since she was going to stop by her mother's after leaving her father's house on Christmas. She planned to get a Starbucks gift card for Aunt Belle's friend and ten-dollar cash cards for his kids since she didn't really know them. Rylan had a thing about everyone she saw and/or planned to spend time with on Christmas day receiving a gift from her. It didn't matter what anyone gave her in return, she just loved the feeling of giving.

"I don't know if we'll be doing all that. But I'm probably going to take off Friday. Got an appointment with my lawyer and a financial advisor."

"Oh?" Rylan asked, concern filling her before her father had a chance to elaborate.

"Yeah. It's time, babygirl. I've had lots of time to think about this and I want us all to start the new year off right. Or at least in the best possible way we can considering the circumstances," he continued.

"What are you saying, Daddy?"

She didn't really want to hear him say it because deep down Rylan already knew. But this conversation had to happen. She took a deep breath and squared her shoulders preparing herself to take what just might be the hardest news of her life.

"The financial guy is doing a valuation of the business. When we meet with the lawyer on Friday, we're gonna talk about how soon it can be sold and what to offer your mother. I want you to have part of the proceeds too, so don't you worry. You'll have a little piece of something to carry you through until you can figure out what your next step is," he said.

Rylan remained quiet.

"I sure wish you were married and had a good man to take care of you, but I know young folk don't aim for that goal anymore."

Will scratched his head again.

"Anyway, you're a smart girl, Rylan. You can go back to school and get yourself a fancy degree. Do something in one of those office buildings they're putting up down at the industrial park. We all have to make changes sometimes, and I guess the time for the Kent family to move on is now."

The pain was different than she'd imagined. It didn't sit in her chest like a boulder or threaten to suffocate her. Instead, Rylan just felt empty. As if a huge part of her life had just slipped away without her doing a damn thing to hold onto it.

Will scrubbed a hand over his cheek and cleared his throat. "So, what I need you to do this morning is get a good estimate on that Lamborghini. If it's still sitting on our lot come next Monday, we're putting it up for sale. The finance guy already advised we liquidate the big assets around here. Once you get the total, send it to my email and I'll send it over to the lawyer. There's plenty of buyers for a car like that, but I figure we can work the sale through the lawyer to keep everything legal and documented."

"You've thought of everything," Rylan said finally.

Will shrugged. "I had to. All this is my fault. So, it was my duty to figure it out."

Rylan nodded, words clogging in her throat alongside the threat of tears.

"Now, don't get emotional. I don't know how much more of this I can take, Rylan. Just let me do the right thing for once. The right thing for all of us. Can you do that?"

Could she? Could she walk away from the place she'd dreamed would one day be hers? Could she stand to the side and watch her father sell off everything he'd ever worked for? Did she have another choice?

Rylan had no idea how she made it through the day or into early evening, but she didn't leave the body shop until after seven that evening. She climbed into her car and drove directly to her mother's house.

It always smelled like potpourri or a bouquet of fresh flowers whenever she walked through the oak colored door and stepped into the front foyer. Her mother was obsessively neat and loved the monochromatic look. So, the beige runner at the front door was for her to wipe her feet before stepping onto the textured oak laminate flooring that she'd had installed just two years ago. Rylan's work boots made a muffled sound as she walked through the open archway and into the living room.

Floor to ceiling windows were on two walls of this area, electronic mini blinds lowered three quarters of the way down so that natural light could pour into the room during the daylight hours. Two off white couches faced each other in the center of the room, two beige fabric French armchairs were on the side in between the couches, forming a perfect square within the room. The rugs in this room were of a beige or very light brown hue, coffee and end tables the same. The one burst of color which was totally out of character but a non-negotiable fixture in the room were Naomi's multiple banners and trophies, crowns and other accolades. A 5x7 picture from Rylan's graduation with both her parents was in the den.

"Hello," Estelle said when she entered the living room. "I wasn't expecting you this evening, Rylan. Naomi and I have already had dinner."

Rylan had been standing near the glass cabinet looking at all of Naomi's awards wondering dismally why she was born so different from the other women in this family.

"Hi Mom," she said softly. "I hadn't planned on stopping by."

Because since her father had been gone, this house seemed colder and less welcome than it had during Rylan's childhood years.

"Well, are you going to just stand there? Because I have some reports to go over before a regional school board meeting tomorrow. If you just came over to stare at the furniture, I can leave you alone."

The way she'd left Rylan alone all her life. Because for Estelle, there was no use trying to deal with the daughter who had no intention of being what Estelle wanted her to be.

"Dad's going to give you what you want," Rylan said and turned slowly to face her mother.

At fifty-eight years old, Estelle was still a stunning woman. This evening she wore soft gray wool pants, a crisp white blouse and her black leather house slippers. This morning before she'd left for work, she'd most likely worn her gray and navy-blue tweed jacket with matching suede ankle boots. Her hair was pulled back into a perfect chignon and she still wore the pearl choker and matching earrings that completed her astute school principal outfit.

"You want the money you claim he owes you and he's going to sell the business he's worked his whole life to build to give it to you," she said.

Her voice was surprisingly even as she spoke. Most likely because Rylan had the last nine hours to go over what she would say to the woman who'd given birth to her. How she would express her profound disappointment in the woman who had once loved Rylan's father.

Estelle gave one quick shake of her head. She lifted an arm and wagged her finger as if she were disciplining one of her students.

"Do not come in here and pass judgment on things you know nothing about," she said to Rylan.

"I know that your cool disdain for my father has created an even bigger wedge in this family. I'm not at all affected by the sale of the place where I've worked since I was seven years old?" Rylan asked.

She was astounded by how evenly her tone matched her mother's. Aside from their skin complexion, Rylan would've sworn she and Estelle had absolutely nothing in common.

"You are the child," Estelle began.

"Not anymore," Rylan countered. "And because you want money that you were only entitled to by the graciousness of my father, I'm the one who'll be out of a job once the body shop sells."

"You could have done anything. You still can do anything, Rylan. Stop being so dramatic."

"Why?" Rylan asked, raising her tone. "Why should I not be

emotional about the prospect of watching my father walk away from his dream and mine?"

"He let me down!" Estelle yelled back.

Her shaking fingers moved to cover her stomach as she took steadying breaths.

"He promised that our love, our family, the life we'd envisioned together would always come first and he lied. Gambling took my place. And nothing I did or said could change that for Will. He walked out on this marriage long before I filed for divorce, so don't you stand there and pretend to know what's been going on in my life for the past ten years because you have no idea," Estelle told her.

Rylan didn't know what to say. This had been the most her mother had ever talked to her about her relationship with her father.

"People make mistakes. Are you really so perfect and so rigid that you can't forgive? He made a mistake. He tried to make amends."

"He kept it a secret. He tried to cover it up so I wouldn't know. If I hadn't asked for a divorce, he probably would never have told me how bad his financial situation was. No, Rylan, I cannot easily forgive that when I was right here all along. I didn't go anywhere and at any point Will could have come to me with what he was going through. He chose not to and I chose to walk away from a man I can never trust with my life or the life of my children again."

"I'm not a child," Rylan insisted.

Estelle's hands fell once again to her side. "Then stop acting like one. Don't come running in here to take up for your precious father when you don't know the whole story. And don't you dare judge me based on the type of woman you've become. Running around in secret with a man who hadn't the decency to come back and take care of his ailing mother. Do you think Delano Greer is going to do any better by you, Rylan? If so, you're as delusional as your father."

Rylan gasped. Her mother's words had taken her completely by surprise.

"You know nothing about my relationship with Del."

Estelle shook her head and chuckled. "And neither do you, babygirl."

The sound of her father's nickname for her in her mother's voice was foreign and made Rylan extremely uncomfortable.

"I shouldn't have come here. You never gave a damn about me. It was always Naomi for you."

"And you for your father. Yes, that's the way the battle lines were drawn in this house." Estelle shrugged. "I won't say I'm proud of that fact, Rylan. But there's no use in crying over the past. You are my daughter and I care very much about your well-being. I believe in your potential to be anything you want. I also hope, for you and your sister, that you both find love and can really be cherished and respected by the man you give your heart to. Just because it didn't work out for your father and I, doesn't mean I don't believe it can work for you. But don't be fooled, Rylan. Don't let sentiment or your desire to keep things in your life the same because it's the only way you feel safe, lead you down the wrong path or into the wrong man's bed. Demand more from him from the start so that in the end, you won't be disappointed."

Rylan couldn't stand any more of this. She wasn't going to listen to advice on her love life from her mother, the woman ending her marriage. Her feet couldn't move fast enough to carry her out of the house and into her car. And when she switched on the ignition and pulled out of the driveway, she drove to the only place she knew that would make her feel better.

Del opened his front door at a little after eight to see Rylan standing on the Santa head-shaped doormat.

"Hey. Are you okay?" he immediately asked because her eyes were brimming with tears and she was rocking side-to-side, her arms folded around herself and the puffy coat she wore.

"No," she whimpered and one tear rolled down her cheek.

His heart nearly stopped.

Del reached for her, wrapping an arm around her shoulders and pulled her inside. He closed and locked the door and then pulled her close. For endless moments they stood there with him holding her tightly in his arms. He had no idea what had happened or when. All he knew for certain was that Rylan Kent didn't cry. He'd seen her fall off bikes and walk away with busted knees and elbows without shedding a tear. She'd climbed trees and jumped fences with the rest of the boys in their neighborhood. And the one time Lance had agreed to race her, Rylan had beat him by two cars, but tripped over her shoelaces at the very end tumbling onto the sidewalk where she busted her lip so badly she had to be rushed to the emergency room to get stitches. And she hadn't shed a tear.

So, seeing her like this wasn't normal for Del. Not as her friend, nor as a man who cared very deeply about her.

She continued to make that quiet whimpering sound, her arms around his waist, holding him as if she were afraid he might let her go. He had absolutely no intention of doing that. He did lean back away from her just enough so that he could touch a finger to her chin and tilt her head up until he could look into her eyes.

"Let's get you out of your coat and we'll go sit down. Okay?"

She nodded.

Del unzipped her coat and pulled the sleeves off each arm. He hung it on the coat rack behind the door and then took her hand, leading her into the living room. They sat on the couch and Rylan shivered. He immediately went to the fireplace and worked to get a fire started. Moments later when he returned to where she was still sitting on the couch, he sat beside her and took her hands in his.

"Tell me what happened," he implored.

After she finished, he had no idea what to say. There'd been rumors floating around town about Mr. Will's gambling and Ms. Estelle putting him out of the house, but Del hated the rumor mill in Providence. He'd been its topic of discussion one time too many, so he tended not to believe everything he heard on a third, fourth, fifth or whatever retelling. And he especially tried to mind his own business. He had enough to worry about with the business and the repairs that were coming to the forefront on the house he owned with his siblings. There was no time to take on anyone else's problems.

But Rylan wasn't just anyone else.

"How much would you need to buy the business from your father?" Del asked because he had no idea how much an auto body shop was worth.

He also didn't know how much money he could offer her since he'd tied up most of his savings in the restaurant. And while he'd made some sound investments while he was living in D.C., he didn't have a number on how much they were worth at the moment.

Rylan sighed heavily. "I went to the bank a month ago and applied for a small business loan. But since I have no collateral, I'd need a twenty-five thousand dollar down payment, or the amount they could offer me without it wouldn't come close to being enough to make the purchase. Besides that, my father refuses to sell to me because he thinks I should get married and let my husband take care of me."

She shook her head. "I mean, I never said I didn't want to get married and have a family. But when I do, I'd like it to be because

I've fallen in love with someone and not because I need a man to help keep a roof over my head. I'm perfectly capable of taking care of myself, I've been doing so for a while now."

Del agreed. She had taken good care of herself, even if she was living in a too small, subpar apartment building likely because she wasn't making enough money at the body shop. She drove an antique car which was great for a collector, but she could probably use something a little more reliable. These were just the things that Del noticed. He had no idea if there was anything else Rylan was going without or sacrificing for this business. The thought briefly crossed his mind to say that this might be a blessing in disguise, but Del knew better. He knew what it was like to have a dream and have it collapse while you were helpless to do anything to stop it.

"And you'll continue to take care of yourself," he told her. "This is going to work out, Rylan. You might not feel that way right now, but it will. And if not with this body shop, then with another. With your own, one that you could build and run the way you want to. You have the education and the training to make it work and I believe you can do it. As for your parents' marriage," Del paused. He could only shake his head at that situation. "That's their problem, not yours. Sure, it affects you, but there's nothing you can do but watch and wait while it plays out."

She was sitting quietly on the chair now. She'd used her free hand to wipe the tears from her face.

"I know," she said with another sigh. "I just feel so helpless and I hate that feeling."

"You're not helpless," Del told her. "You have the power to do whatever you want to do to make your life better."

His mother had told him that and though it had taken him a while, Del wholeheartedly believed it.

When Rylan only nodded, Del leaned forward. He untied and removed her boots and then lay back on the couch, pulling her against him. Reaching back to the end table, he handed her the remote to the television.

"It's your choice tonight," he said before kissing the top of her head.

She accepted the remote and snuggled back against him. "I'm gonna need an action movie tonight. No wonderfully cheerful Christmas movie's going to help my mood," she told him, her tone not as light as normal, but not as dismal as it'd been when she first arrived.

A few moments later Del grinned when she leaned forward and set the remote on the floor. She'd left the channel on *Die Hard*.

"Perfect!" she exclaimed as she lay back against him.

Del kept his arms wrapped tightly around her and continued to smile minutes after her comment, because she was absolutely correct. This, right here at this very moment, was perfect.

13

*C*hristmas was five days away and Del still hadn't gotten Rylan a gift.

She and Camy had been shopping for the past two weeks. Del had no idea how many gifts they had to buy but was certain it was way too many. The brothers had already made plans to spend Christmas Eve at Camy's for a game night mixed with more caroling. Del wasn't looking forward to the singing part but had to admit they'd had a great time at his house decorating last weekend. He'd actually enjoyed the whole festive atmosphere more than he imagined he could have again.

It had been a perfect mood changer to get him through the bulk of this week. But tomorrow he would be heading to Washington D.C. to testify in the case of the District of Columbia versus Renaldo Wimbley. That, Del definitely wasn't looking forward to. And yet, he desperately wanted to get it over with.

Del hadn't told Rylan about the trial or that he'd be in D.C. all day tomorrow giving his testimony. He'd considered it. Especially after she'd come to him on Monday evening pouring out all her feelings and concerns about her parents' declining relationship and the pain of losing her father's body shop. As they'd lay on that couch watching one movie after another, Del had thought that he should give her something in return for opening up to him. He should tell her everything about the situation with Shannen and the case that had destroyed his career. But he hadn't.

Instead, they'd ordered pizza and after eating until they were stuffed, headed upstairs to bed. They'd slept in Del's bed cuddled together just as they had been on the couch and it had felt more than right to Del. It felt as if it were meant to be. Getting up the next morning, Del rode with Rylan because his truck was ready to be picked-up. He'd been more than happy to call the rental company and have the second SUV picked up once and for all.

Now, he was overseeing a few deliveries that they'd wanted to get in before Christmas. Jeret and Rock were off this morning, so it was just Del, Lance and Ethan on the lower level. Noah was in the back office dreaming up more marketing strategies for the bar. One of which included an endorsement proposal they planned to pitch to Ellis Colby once they hosted his and Naomi's engagement party. With that thought in mind, Del pulled his phone out of his back pocket and was scrolling through his contacts for Naomi's number so he could confirm the meeting with her and the event planner she'd hired for the first week in January. They'd played a bit of phone tag throughout the week, but Del wanted to get this date nailed down before next week when everyone would be busy with holiday plans and Ethan and Portia's upcoming wedding. Unfortunately, he'd had to leave Naomi another message.

Del had just disconnected the call when he looked up to see Mal walking proudly through the front door.

His body tensed at the sight, but Del took deep, slow breaths to remain calm. He took a few steps until he was out from behind the bar and standing near one of the empty tables. It was just after noon, so the bar wouldn't start to fill up until around four when the happy hour crowd poured in.

Mal walked directly toward Del, which wasn't that much of a surprise. The guy loved confrontation. What did give Del a little pause was the fact that Mal wasn't alone. Sheriff Mike Johansen walked just a few steps behind him.

They'd walked right past the hostesses, so Del did the honors.

"Afternoon," he said with a nod. "You guys need a table or will you be sitting at the bar?"

Mal's slowly spreading smile said they had another reason for being here.

"Hey Del," Mike said and reached a hand around where Mal stood.

Del shook the guy's hand. They'd met immediately after Del returned to Providence when Del had visited the Sheriff's office to let the man know that he was no longer with the DEA and would be living in Providence again. It wasn't something he was required to do, but Del had felt it was a common courtesy. He got the feeling the handshake was Mike's way of doing the same.

"I wasn't sure if you heard, but Renaldo Wimbley's body was found in a motel over in Denton. Murder." Mike continued.

Del hadn't known. The notification of Wimbley's death wasn't a surprise—the guy was a drug kingpin who'd made enemies in every state across the nation, not to mention a few international ones. Some would say his death by some form of violence was karma. Del just figured it was a way of life.

"I hadn't heard that," Del told him. "Thanks for coming all the way over here to inform me know."

"I know you were supposed to testify up in D.C. tomorrow, so I figured you'd like to know you wouldn't need to make that trip," Mike said. "Looks good in here."

"Thanks, again," Del said and waited. These two wanted something more than to deliver a personal message that would save him a drive to D.C. in the morning. And even if Mike was giving Del another professional courtesy by personally delivering that news, Mal had no business coming in with him to gloat.

Mal's eyes almost glittered with excitement. The guy was rocking back on the heels of his worn loafers, hands stuffed in the front pockets of his khaki pants.

"Yeah, so you don't have to go to D.C., but you are going somewhere," Mal said. "To a place I've known you always belonged. And as soon as you're gone, I'm going to petition the council to have this place shut down for good."

Del looked away from Mal and back to Mike for the rest of the explanation.

The sheriff reached into his back pocket and pulled out some folded papers. He extended it to Del and said, "I've got a warrant to search your truck and your house."

Mike had lowered his voice when he said that and Del appreciated the man's tact in this still puzzling situation. As for Mal, well, Del would continue to bite down on the urge to kick his bony ass all around this bar.

"Hey, Mike. What's up?" Lance asked as he came over to join them.

Del had taken the papers, unfolded them and was now reading over the warrant. They were looking for anything that connected him to Renaldo Wimbley and a 2016 red Lamborghini Aventador.

"Hey Lance. Ah, I'm just tying up some loose ends on an investigation," Mike said.

"What investigation? I haven't seen Wimbley in almost two years and I have no idea whose car this is," Del said.

"Let me see that," Lance said before taking the papers from Del's hand.

"You're going down now, Greer," Mal taunted.

"I'm calling our attorney," Lance said.

"I'm going to ask you to come with me, Del," Mike said.

"Am I being arrested?" he asked.

Mike immediately shook his head. "No. Right now we just want to talk about your interactions with Wimbley. You can grab your jacket and ride with me over to your place. I'll have one of my deputies pick up your truck, if you want to give me your keys so they won't have to impound it."

Because if people in town saw that his truck was being impounded, they would assume he was in trouble. Again.

"He's not going anywhere with you," Lance announced. "And you, you little prick, don't you ever get tired of creating stories?"

Del moved to his right, blocking Lance from Mal. He dug into his pocket and pulled out his keys. After removing the key to the truck, he handed it over to Mike.

"Lance will drive me to my place," Del stated evenly. "And you will get the hell out of my bar. Now," he said to Mal. "And don't come back."

Mal laughed but he didn't move. "Gladly," he said. "But you don't have to worry about me coming back because there'll be nothing to come back to."

Three hours later, Del stood in his living room amid the holiday decorations and Rylan's burgundy sweater which she'd left hanging over the back of the couch. Lance stood with his arms folded near the fireplace while Noah, Jeret, Rock and Ethan were either sitting or standing somewhere in the room as well.

"What the hell do we have to do for people in this town to believe we've changed?" Rock asked. "I mean, damn. We graduate from high school without any of us serving jail time. We head off to college or the military and all of us went into damn good careers. Now we're back running a great restaurant and giving back to the community and it's still not enough. What the hell do they want from us? Blood?"

"They want us gone," Ethan said solemnly. "Bastards."

"Well that's just too damn bad," Noah stated evenly. "We belong here just as much as Mal Penning with his sniveling spoiled ass!"

Lance nodded. "We should've beat him into the concrete when we had the chance."

Jeret sighed. "That was fifteen years ago."

"And it wouldn't have stopped him from becoming the bitch-ass monster he is now," Del told them.

He ran a hand down the back of his head and sighed. Renaldo Wimbley was found in a motel in Denton, which was located just about an hour and a half west of Providence. He'd been holed up there since the end of October when he'd dropped his Lamborghini off at Kent Automotive to be serviced. Mike figured Wimbley knew Del was back in Providence and was planning to make a move on him using his car breaking down as a cover. But he never came back to get the car because someone had entered the motel room one night while Wimbley slept and shot him ten times in the face.

"Can't believe Mr. Will pointed him in your direction," Jeret said. "I'd think he knew you were a better man than that, especially since you've been dating Rylan."

Del's jaw clenched at those words because that's precisely what he was trying to figure out. He wanted answers and he only knew one way to get them.

Rylan had just stepped out of her car and was heading back into the shop to finish up some paperwork she'd left when Camy called about them doing more shopping. She'd only meant to go to the one store that they'd forgotten to go to last night but ended up staying out for over three hours. Now, she was crossing the parking lot with quick steps as the Lamborghini was being towed by a truck with the sheriff's department logo on the side.

"What's going on?" she asked her father who was standing at the front door of the shop, a deep scowl on his face.

"Did you know that car belonged to a drug kingpin?" Will asked in return.

Stunned, Rylan stared at her father and then back to the car. "No. I mean, I don't usually ask for occupation when they bring in their cars. He gave me a name, cell phone number and email address. That's all we needed for our forms."

Will was shaking his head. "Now we can kiss any money coming in from that direction good-bye. The car's being impounded by the cops because the drug dealer turned up dead over in Denton."

"What? Oh my goodness," Rylan said.

She would've never imagined that this would be the result of her dealings with Lamborghini Guy. He'd seemed like a normal man when he'd come in and dropped the car off, even though Rylan had briefly wondered why he wasn't taking a car like that to a specialty dealer. She wasn't about to turn away the huge profit they'd expected to make from working on it, so she hadn't asked him that question. But now it was gone.

Oh well, she thought and moved around her father to go inside. They wouldn't have the shop much longer anyway, so she wasn't going to stress over losing their fee. Besides, she'd just found the perfect gift for Del and she was like a kid filled with excitement as she waited for Christmas Day.

Rylan was inside the waiting area of the shop by the time she heard the tow truck pull off. Her father had stepped inside and walked on back to his office without saying another word to her.

Rylan was still standing at the front desk going through their mail when Del came in.

"Hey, you!" she said when she looked up and quickly moved around the desk intending to give him a hug.

But she stopped just a few steps away from him when she noted the angry glare in his eyes.

"What's going on?" she asked when dread circled in the pit of her stomach.

"You kept my truck here longer than you first said you needed to," he said through clenched teeth.

It was Rylan's turn to frown. "I told you, our supplier couldn't get the part on time."

"And when I told you about Shannen, you never once thought it might be nice to tell me you had Renaldo Wimbley's car here? That the bastard that killed Shannen and cost me my job had been here in town? In this shop?"

Rylan took a step back. Not out of fear, but because her mind was reeling now as she tried to figure out what Del was saying.

"You told me about Shannen just last week. And you didn't mention anything about anyone named Renaldo Wimbley. I don't even know who that is," she said slowly. "Del, tell me what's happened? First, I get here and one of our biggest accounts receivable is being hauled off by the cops. My father's pissed because that's money lost and now, you're in here looking like you're about to explode. I'm just trying to catch up here."

"So, they took the car. What the hell did you think was going to happen? I'm lucky I wasn't arrested after your father told them that I had Wimbley's car as well as my truck here to hide them from the cops. Oh, and that's exactly why they thought I killed Wimbley, because obviously we'd been working together all along. How else could I have walked away from the DEA and come here to open a restaurant?"

Now, she was confused and getting angry. "Wait, my father did what?"

"He told the cops that I was working with a drug kingpin! The sheriff came into the bar to serve me with a search warrant. They went through my truck and my house but found nothing because I'm not a criminal. But obviously your father feels differently."

He'd started pacing at that point and Rylan could only stare at him. Was she hearing all this correctly? Had her father done this to him and if so, why?

"I should've known better!" he yelled. "I knew it was a mistake. I should've stayed the hell away from you on a personal level. If Will didn't want me with his darling daughter, all he had to do was say so!"

His words were harsh and slapped at her as if they were a physical attack. Whatever confusion or anger she'd begun to feel about this situation was now replaced by fury. Knowing it was best to put some distance between her and Del at this point, she moved back again, until she was once again behind the desk.

"Del, I really don't know what's happening right now. But it might be a good idea if you go home and cool down. I'll talk to my dad to get a clearer story."

"I just gave you the story!" Del yelled.

He crossed the room until he stood directly in front of her.

"I was almost arrested; do you understand what that means? Pencil-neck Mal was all but running to the city council to tell them that I was up to my old tricks again and use that as a reason to shut the restaurant down. I could've lost everything because of you and your father!" he shouted.

Rylan blinked and prayed that the tears stinging the backs of her eyes didn't fall. Was he serious? Did he really think her father had intentionally tried to sabotage him and his friends?

"First, you need to step back outta my face and then you

should really lower your tone. I'm not one of your suspects that you can berate and scream at to get the answers you want." Her body was shaking with rage at this point, and another emotion she didn't want to deal with right now. "Better yet, you should definitely leave before this situation gets any worse." She didn't even know how that was possible, but what she did know was that she wasn't about to stand here and take this crap from him, especially since she still didn't know what the hell he was talking about.

Now it was his turn to take a step back as if he'd been slapped. He took a deep breath and she could see him struggling to release it slowly, to calm down perhaps. But really, it was probably too late for that.

"Look," he started, his voice at a lower and more even tone now. "I'm sorry for yelling, but I need answers. Why would you and your father set me up like that? You had to know what the consequences would be."

Rylan could only stare at him as her heart thumped in her chest. She was glad it was thumping instead of actually breaking which was what she knew would happen the moment he walked out.

"What you're not going to do is stand here and blame me for something I know nothing about. Whatever you've gotten yourself into in the past that's now come back to haunt you, is your thing, Del. Not mine or my father's and I'm beyond offended that you would even come in here spouting that type of nonsense."

"This is my life, Rylan. My business, my brothers' business, all that we've worked for is the most important thing to me."

And she was nothing. She was the woman who he'd been sleeping with for the past few weeks, but who ultimately meant nothing to him.

"I don't have what you need, Del," she said and felt a sort of finality to those words. "I obviously never did."

Del ran his hands down the back of his head and sighed again.

"Rylan, listen," he started to say.

She was already shaking her head. "No. I'm not going to do that," she told him. "I want you out of my shop. Now."

She had no idea how she managed to keep her tone so calm and serious when inside she was raging, but it had Del blinking twice before dropping his hands to his side. He opened his mouth to say something else, but she went to the door and held it open, waiting for him to walk out of it. And out of her life.

He stared at her for another few seconds before shaking his head and leaving. Rylan inhaled deeply as he passed, getting a whiff of his cologne and resisting the urge to cry out.

What had happened?

Why had it happened?

And what the hell was she supposed to do with all the feelings that had been building inside her these past few weeks? How was she supposed to deal with the fact that the man she was in love with had just accused her of setting him up?

14

"What did you tell the sheriff about Del?" Rylan asked her father twenty minutes after Del had walked out.

It had taken her that amount of time to get herself together before initiating this confrontation. While she'd been boiling with anger about the entire situation, the sting of Del's cruel accusations had gripped her heart in a vice that she hadn't immediately been able to break free of. She wasn't feeling totally better at this moment but the questions surrounding this circumstance needed answers. Whether or not those answers would assuage any of the hurt and disappointment she was feeling right now, she wasn't sure.

Her father had been sitting behind the old scuffed up desk he'd insisted on keeping in his small office toward the back of the body shop. He looked older and a bit thinner in the seconds it took for him to fold his hands on top of the desk and lift his rheumy eyes to her. "I didn't tell the sheriff anything about your boyfriend. Even though you neglected to tell me you were sleeping with one of those Greer boys you used to like hanging around so much."

She shook her head. "I hung around with Camy, not her brothers. And that doesn't matter. What matters right now is that Del thinks you told the sheriff that he was keeping that car here. He thinks we set him up!" Her chest heaved with those last words, fury and pain wrestling for dominance in her mind.

Her father stood and pushed his chair back. "Now wait a minute. Just calm down and tell me exactly what you're talking about."

"No, Daddy, you tell me what's going on here. Tell me why the man I've been involved with just accused me of doing something I'd never think of doing to him, or to anyone for that matter. Tell me what you told the sheriff about him."

"First of all, the sheriff came to see me about half an hour after I opened the shop this morning. I didn't know what the hell was going on, not until he mentioned he'd gotten a tip about that car being here," Will told her.

"I don't understand," she said still trying to make sense of this crazy situation that was ripping her heart in pieces. "Who'd tell the sheriff about a car being serviced in our shop and why? Were they looking for the car?" If it belonged to a well-known drug dealer that was definitely a possibility. Maybe she would start asking the occupation of their customers now, or at least requesting a work number under the pretense of needing an alternative way of contacting customers about their vehicles.

"I thought it was odd too because it was the second time in two days somebody'd been in here asking about the car. Somebody other than the owner who still owed us a ton of money for fixing that fancy thing."

"The second time?" she asked. "Who else had come in asking about the car?"

He shrugged. "Mal Penning came in last night just before closing. You'd already left and I was just about to lock up when he pulled into the parking lot. I thought something might've been wrong with his car again. You know he doesn't know how to drive a stick."

Rylan suddenly had a sick feeling in the pit of her stomach. "What did Mal want?"

"Just small talk. Said he was thinking about trading his car in for a newer model or possibly an SUV." Will stopped then. He dragged a hand down the back of his head, a similar motion to what Del had done in her office a while ago. "Shit. Mal said he was thinking about getting an SUV like Del's."

Realization settled over her slowly. "Del hadn't picked up his truck yet, but we'd moved it outside to the parking lot so we could pull that Acura in to be worked on today and because Del was coming to get his truck this morning." She'd been with Del last night after work and she'd told him the truck was ready. Since she'd been spending more nights at his place than her own, they'd decided that instead of coming to pick up the truck last night, they'd just ride to the shop together this morning and he'd get it then. Which he had, and then they'd kissed longingly, neither of them wanting to part but knowing they'd had to get started with their workday and had reluctantly done so. If she weren't so pissed off right now, she'd cry with the bittersweet sentiment that memory brought to mind.

"I still had the bay doors open when he was here and he walked over and started asking about the car. Price, how it ran, and stuff like that. I didn't think anything of it," Will said.

Rylan could only shake her head as the pieces to this puzzle began to slowly fall into place. "Mal still hates Del. He hates that Del broke his nose and made a fool of him fifteen years ago and hates that Mel and his brothers are back now making something out of the bar." But she'd never thought that hate would go this far. And besides that, she had no clue how Mal knew who that Lamborghini belonged to and how it connected to Del's case.

"I thought that was kid stuff and they'd both grown out of it." Will came around the desk to stand in front of her. "They've both got good jobs now and really have no need to butt heads. At least not that I know of. I mean, sure, Mal and his daddy can be assholes. Everybody in town knows they're racist bastards." But they'd had no choice but to bring their cars into Kent Automotive for service or take them into the next town more than fifty miles away, so they'd each been in here on numerous occasions, giving fake smiles but signing checks that cleared.

"Mal's father is the district attorney," she said, wondering if that meant anything in this situation. Of course, it did and her fists clenched with the knowledge. "I bet that's how he knew the authorities were looking for that car and once he saw it here, he went running to the sheriff to tell. Mal would do anything to get back at Del." And he'd done it, finally. Only Del thought it had been her and her father.

"Okay, okay, I see what's happened here." He father took her by the shoulders. "You listen to me. I'm gonna go right over to Del's place and clear the air. I'll tell him what I told Sheriff Johansen and why. I'll fix this for you, babygirl. I will."

But Rylan's eyes were already welling with tears. She took deep breaths and shook her head willing those tears not to fall. "No. There's nothing for you to fix for me," she told him. "I'm not the one in trouble with the law."

"No," her father said, "But your heart's in trouble. I can see it on your face. And now you're shaking. It's my fault and I'm gonna fix it."

"No, Daddy. It's not your fault. Del didn't have to come storming in here saying the things he said to me." If he'd loved... no, if he'd trusted her, he wouldn't have.

She was a fool. Del had never said those words to her and she hadn't thought she wanted to hear them. Sure, he'd been hurt and confused himself, but he'd also been intentionally mean and judgmental and that's what bothered her more. A part of her wanted to run over to his place right now and tell him what a colossal ass he'd been blaming her and believing she could do such a thing, but she wouldn't. Pride kept her from doing anything else to make a fool of herself for a man she should've never been with in the first place.

"I'm gonna go home now," she said with a wavering smile to her father.

"Listen to me, Rylan. I'm gonna go and clear the air with him. If what I said did something to get him into trouble, I want him to know why I said it. That's what a man does when he makes a mistake."

"You didn't make a mistake, Daddy. You had no idea what Mal was up to. Hell, I'm not even sure I know all the ins and outs to what happened." She blinked furiously because those stupid tears definitely wanted to fall. "And you know what, it doesn't matter. This feud between Mal and Del has nothing to do with me." And whatever she'd thought was between Del had been a mistake, his actions today had made that perfectly clear.

Rylan was home alone on Christmas Eve.

The medium-size tree Del had purchased for her stood in between the dining and living room portion of her apartment, decorated with multi-colored lights and ornaments. The all-day, all-Christmas radio station played holiday tunes and she'd turned it up when *The Christmas Song* had come on about half an hour ago. So, her music was loud when she answered the door wearing thermal winter wonderland pajamas and thick red socks.

"Merry Christmas, babygirl."

Her father stood on the other side of the door smiling at her. Rylan didn't return the smile. She wasn't in the mood for company. Hadn't been for the past couple of days.

"Hi Dad," she replied because to continue standing there in silence was rude.

"Can I come in?"

Rylan stepped to the side. She hadn't wanted any company and had hoped that he would come to that conclusion by her lack of invitation. Obviously, that wasn't the case.

"I'm really tired," she began as she closed her door and noticed her father going deeper into the apartment until stopping in the dining room. "I was going to finish wrapping a few things and then turn in early."

"I won't take much of your time," he said and dropped a folder onto the round table.

Rylan tried not to sigh with exasperation. She really was tired of talking to people this week. No matter how well meaning they thought they were being, she was just talked out.

"I thought about some things you've said in the past weeks," he told her.

She stopped a few feet away from him, folding her arms over her chest. "And what was that?"

Rylan had said a lot to her father since that awful day last week. She'd already questioned him after Del left the shop in a rage that day and she'd gotten most of the answers to a very unfortunate situation. In the time since then Camy had come to her apartment, then to the shop and she'd called numerous times a day giving her bits and pieces of more things they'd found out about Mal and his twisted intentions against Del. But she sensed her father was talking about something different.

"You've said a lot," he replied and then chuckled. "Most of it I needed to hear. And some I guess you were saying out of hurt." Will lowered his head. He stared at his feet for a moment and then looked over to the Christmas tree. "This used to be the most wonderful time of the year," he said.

Boy did it, she thought but refused to speak.

"I talked to my lawyer and the finance man on Friday, just like I'd planned," he continued. "I had them draw these papers up. Told them I needed them right away, before Christmas."

"If you want me to review the sale papers, Dad, that's fine but I can't do it until next Monday. I'm taking this week off."

She needed a month or two off, in another town, or perhaps another country.

"No. I don't need you to go over the papers. I told the finance guy what I wanted to do and he gave me some numbers. Then I had the lawyer draw up these papers transferring the body shop to you."

Rylan wasn't sure she heard him correctly. "What did you say?"

"I'm giving you the body shop," he said. "Minus a few of those older tools I liked to use while you preferred to work strictly with the computer on some problems. And the Pontiac."

She was shaking her head as she moved to the table and lifted the envelope. Rylan pulled out the stack of papers and flipped through them. They were deed transfers for the land and corporation transfers.

"Wait, you sold the Pontiac?"

The 1969 GTO had been one of her father's first cars. He'd pampered that car more than he had his children.

He nodded. "Yep. My finance guy bought it," he replied with a chuckle. "Those proceeds were enough to pay off all the body shop debt. I still have to work on my personal debt, but at least the body shop is free and clear."

He was right, that's what she read during her quick perusal of the papers. "But why? Why would you sell the Pontiac now, when you didn't do it to bail yourself out before?"

He shrugged. "Pride, I guess. I kept thinking I could fix things without sacrificing what I already had. But then I lost my wife and Naomi, she hasn't really talked to me much since I moved out. After you and I talked about that misunderstanding with Del, I knew that if I went forward with the deal to sell the place that I might lose you too."

Rylan's chest hurt. She set the papers down and touched a hand to her father's arm. "I told you that stuff with Del wasn't your fault, Daddy. Besides, you can never lose me."

Will leaned in and kissed her on top of her head. "I almost did. I saw it in your eyes that day. You felt like you were losing everything, all the things that had made you happy, and I didn't want any part of that."

"Last week, well on that day last week, it wasn't about you. Del had said some things and..." she stopped. She didn't want to talk about this anymore. "Thank you! Thank you so much for trusting me with this."

She wrapped her arms around her father's shoulders and hugged him tightly. Will hugged her in return. "Thank you for wanting it as much as I used to," he whispered.

When they pulled away, Will tweaked her nose the way he used to when she was younger.

"Now, why are you sitting in here alone on Christmas Eve? Didn't you tell me you had plans to be with Camy tonight?"

Because he still had his arms around her Rylan couldn't turn away. She could, however, shake her head. "No plans."

"No plans, or you canceled the plans because of what happened with Del?"

Rylan didn't respond.

"Uh huh, I thought so. Look, babygirl, I told you that Del and I spoke. We ironed everything out. That arrogant little snot, Mal ran straight to the sheriff twisting our conversation around to make it seem like Del had asked us to hide the car for him."

Rylan nodded. "I know. Sheriff Johansen came to see me to tell me that's how he got the warrant so quickly. Because Mal had talked to you and knew that Del's truck and the Wimbley car was there. He didn't question it since news of the Wimbley murder had just come through. But later after they found nothing at Del's house, he sat Mal down and threatened him with perjury."

"That lying little weasel," Will said.

"And Camy told me that Mal's father had been in contact with Del's boss for a while because he'd wanted to check up on the real reason why Del left the DEA. And since Del's boss was afraid of what Del might say on the witness stand, he shared his own version of what happened to make Del resign." She sighed because it had all been so much. For days she'd felt like she was involved in some type of drama reality show.

"Hope they toss all the liars in a jail cell, starting with Mal," Will said with a huff.

She shrugged. "They might. The sheriff said he was going to get to the bottom of everything. I heard the FBI's involved now too."

"And none of this has anything to do with what you and Del were building together," her father added.

"That's done," she told him in a resolute tone and moved out of his grasp this time.

"Doesn't have to be."

"He doesn't want me. He never did. It was all just a...misunderstanding," she said quietly. "And I don't want to talk about it anymore. You want some hot chocolate?"

Will nodded and took off his jacket. "Let me just say this one thing and then you can go into that kitchen and fix us some hot chocolate. When you have love, real and true love, in the palm of your hand. You need to close up your fingers and hold on to it as tight as you can."

He'd crossed to her, taken her hand and demonstrated his words.

"Don't let it slip away, Rylan. Don't ever let it slip away."

Del was in a room full of people on Christmas Eve. And yet he'd never felt as alone as he did at this very moment.

He blamed that on the fact that he was the weakest link on his team and they were down fifteen points in the trivia game Camy had insisted they play. When Noah, Jeret and Rock finally got tired of him missing the answers they unanimously decided to evict him from the team. So, he'd left the living room where everyone was sitting around laughing, drinking and having a good time, and went into the dining room.

He sat at the old cherrywood table and toyed with the same white lace tablecloth that his mother used to pull out at Christmastime. When he grew tired of doing that, he reached into his pocket to retrieve his phone. No text messages. He logged into the social media app. No messages.

He sighed heavily.

"You two have got to be the most stubborn people in all of the state of Virginia," Camy said when she walked in carrying a tray with empty glasses.

"Not now, Camelia," Del snapped.

He should've known better.

Camy set the tray on the table hard enough to make the glasses clink.

"Listen here, Delano Gerald Greer," she said putting her hands on her hip.

Del groaned and let his head fall back. He was in trouble now. She'd pulled out the full name and followed up with hands on hips. If Lance were in his position, Del would laugh with glee at the tongue lashing he knew was coming. As his brother wasn't the one on the hot seat right now, Del could only sit there and take it since it was his fault for coming over here when he knew he wasn't in the mood for people.

"I'm not the one who kept a lot of the details about the situation with this Wimbley guy and the court testimony a secret. If you'd trusted Rylan enough to tell her what was really going on, she probably would've been better prepared when the police showed up at the body shop. And maybe if you hadn't run to the body shop after that, shouting accusations at her, she wouldn't be ghosting your ass right now. But no, that's too much like right. You always have to do things your way, which a good amount of time isn't the right way. And now, you're gonna sit here and wallow in your broken heart instead of heading over to Rylan's place to talk to her."

"One, I do not have a broken heart and two, I'm right more than half the time," he said.

Camy tilted her head and lifted her lips into a smirk. "In your mind. Look, Del, Rylan is in love with you."

"How do you know that?" He and Rylan had never talked about their feelings for each other. Not before the Mal and his attempt to have Del tossed in jail, and certainly not after all that crap went down.

"Because she's my best friend. And if you could see past your own foolishness about relationships and work, you would've seen it too. You blindsided her with all your accusations and you hurt her by saying you should've known not to get involved with her as if her and her father had somehow embarrassed you," she said. "That was low and it was bullshit. You've known Rylan and her family all her life. Besides that, she's the closest thing I've ever had to a sister. Did you really think she could do something like that to hurt my brother knowing how that would affect me and our friendship?"

He felt like an ass. Actually, he'd had a week to get used to that feeling. From the moment he'd left the body shop that day, after seeing the dismissive look in her eyes, he'd realized his mistake. Now, he could only shake his head because most of everything Camy had just said, he'd already told himself on more than one occasion. "That wasn't how I meant it," was all he managed to say.

Camy frowned. "Then you should've stayed there and told her that."

"She wanted me to leave." She'd said it twice and each time the words had sliced coldly through his heart because he'd known she meant for him to leave the place he'd taken up in her life, not just for him to physically get out of her shop.

"And you wanted to leave?" Camy didn't wait for his reply, but instead came around the table and sat in the chair beside him. "You want to be with her, I can see it. Everybody in this house right now can see it. And I know she wants to be with you even though I swear that girl gives a new meaning to the word stubborn. Why do you think she's not here now?"

Del scrunched his face. "That doesn't make sense. If she wanted to be with me, why not come to where she knows I am."

She punched him in the arm.

"Ow, what was that for?"

"For breaking a record and saying the dumbest shit in the past week. She's not here for the same reason you haven't crawled back to her with apologies dripping from your mouth."

Del sighed because he knew his sister was absolutely right. "It's too late. I screwed up and she has every right not to want to see me again. So, we'll all just go back to the way we were before."

"You think it's that simple? It's not," she said.

Portia came into the room at that moment. "She's right. It's not that simple."

He looked from Portia to Camy wondering how the hell women could do that secret communicating thing.

"Then I don't know what else to do," he admitted and heard the hush that immediately fell over the room.

"Is that the captain admitting he doesn't know what to do?" Ethan came in wrapping his arms around Portia's waist and pulling her back against him.

"Wait? Del's admitting defeat? I gotta see this for myself," Jeret said.

Before he could blink again, everyone who was in the living room was now in the dining room with him. He would've huffed and got up to leave, but it felt good to look into the faces of the people who loved him most in the world. It felt damn good.

"Yeah, okay, I'm admitting it. I want her back, but I don't know how to do it. So, since you're all standing here professing to have some sort of knowledge in matters of the heart, let me hear it," he said. "But I'm warning you, if you make me look bad, I'll never forgive any of you."

"How can we possibly make you look any worse than you already do?" Lance asked and then cracked up laughing.

The others followed suit, until Camy quieted them down and began talking seriously. Del listened. He contemplated and he planned. He was going to get Rylan back because life without her just wasn't worth living.

*T*wo days after Christmas, Rylan walked into Game Changers at a little after two in the morning. She hadn't been here in almost two weeks and was resigned to keep it that was for even longer, until she'd received the text from Camy.

Camy: Had way too many Candy Cane Vodkas at the bar. Need a ride home cause the guys are being mean to me.

The guys probably weren't being mean at all, maybe chastising because they didn't like Camy or any woman at their bar getting pissy drunk. Rock had several Uber drivers on speed dial so that anyone at the bar, especially women, who weren't able to drive, could get home safely. Where Camy was concerned, any one of the brothers would've gladly taken her home and preached to her about the stupidity of drinking too much the entire time, which was probably why Rylan had received the text.

Why she'd been awake and staring at her ceiling so that she'd grabbed her phone as soon as it buzzed, was nobody's business.

She got out of her car, closed and locked the door and walked across the almost empty parking lot toward the side entrance of the bar. They were closing in a few minutes, but the door was probably locked so she was prepared to bang on it when it opened for her instead.

"Hey," Del said a quick smile on his face.

That smile, his eyes, the breadth of his chest and the scent of his cologne were all things she hadn't seen or smelled in while. It took her mind and her body a moment to adjust to the surprise and the memory. Truth be told, she'd been living with the memories of Del daily as if they were her new uninvited houseguest. "Hey," she said back to him. "I'm here to pick up Camy."

"Come on in," he replied and pushed the door open wider, standing with his back against it so she could step inside.

It had snowed again last night leaving a couple feet on the ground and frigid temperatures in the air, so she wasn't about to make any foolish statements like, "No, I'll wait out here." She did, however, make a concerted effort to not touch him as she stepped into the bar. She also held her breath because her body wasn't doing so good not reacting to the scent of his cologne, that tugging in her chest she'd started feeling whenever he was near had returned with full force.

That sensation slipped her mind when she noticed the bar was completely empty and dark, but for the candles illuminating one of the tables closest to the wall. Music played lightly, an instrumental version of an R&B song she knew but couldn't name at the moment. She spun around when she heard the door close. "What's going on? Where's Camy?"

"She's home," Del said stepping out of the shadows of the doorway into the glow of light afforded by the candles. "She said to tell you she's really sorry, but it was for a good cause."

His tone was light, but her heart was beating frantically. "What was for a good cause? Lying to me?"

The moment she said those words, Rylan glanced at the candles again and then back to Del. She was gonna strangle Camy. The moment she left here she was going to her house and banging on the door until either she opened it, or all the neighbors woke up ready to curse her out for the disturbance.

"It's too late for games," she said and started back toward the door.

Del reached out, grasping her arm to stop her. "Wait. Please," he said softly.

She didn't look over at him, but she didn't keep walking either. "I'm not somebody you and your sister can toy with. I was in bed asleep thinking I was coming to help a friend."

"You came to see a friend," he said. "At least I hope we're still friends."

Rylan did turn her head to stare at him then. "Oh come on, Del. Tell me you didn't call me here in the middle of the night to give me the "let's be friends" speech."

He let his hand fall from her arm, probably assured that she wasn't going to run out at this moment since she'd stopped to talk to him again. "No, Rylan. I wanna be so much more than just friends with you."

She opened her mouth to say something and he held up a hand to stop her. "But I'm not pressing that issue right now. Tonight, I just wanted to talk to you. To clear the air."

Inhaling deeply wasn't meant as any kind of play on his words, she just needed to take a breath, to reinforce the vow she'd made to herself to get on with her life without him.

"Look, I know everything that happened and I know that you were upset that day. If I were in your shoes I would've been upset too." She wouldn't have gone to his house blaming him for her troubles though. "So, there's no need for us to discuss it any further."

"You're wrong," he said with a shake of his head. "I owe you so much more than a discussion."

"You don't owe me anything. We're adults, we decided to do a thing for a while and now it's done." She did take a step to get away from him at that point because try as she had over the past days, she hadn't yet mastered convincing herself that what they'd had was over.

"Please don't go." He didn't touch her this time, just stated that simple plea. "You don't have to talk. But I'm asking you to stay and listen."

Rylan knew she should keep walking. "You're asking me to stand here and listen when all I wanted from you that day was for you to stop accusing me and my father of trying to hurt you but you refused to do that."

"I was an idiot. I was angry and hurt and I know those aren't excuses. They're just the truth. And despite what I may or may not have done in my past, Rylan, you know I've never lied to you."

He hadn't. Not even when one of the guys on the football team had called her flat-chested when she'd come to one of their games. Del had jacked the guy up by the collar of his shirt and made him apologize to her, but after the guy had run off she'd asked him if he'd thought she was flat-chested and Del, with his cute half-smile had replied, "Yeah, you kinda are, but you can run laps around that jerk on the track.". She'd agreed with him that day and he'd walked her home, cracking jokes and making her laugh all the way. Pain seared through her chest at the memory.

"I was wrong and I'm sorry. I should've known better. I should've been calmer."

She spun around again. "You should've trusted me."

He nodded. "You're right, I should've."

"Why didn't you? Because I've never lied to you either, Del."

"I'm not used to trusting people," he replied. "When I was a kid, I trusted that my parents would always be together and they'd always be there for me, but that didn't happen. My dad died and then my mom was gone. I trusted the counselors at school who said to be honest and things would be alright, so I convinced Lance that we should admit to trashing those bathrooms. And we got thrown into Grace House. Then I trusted that we were all equal and had the same rights as every other kid in this town, but then Mal came onto the basketball court that day and talked all that trash before calling my mother names." He stopped, scrubbed his hands over his face and stared at her. "Yeah, I broke his nose, but he deserved that and so much more. They gave me more time at the House and that's when I realized I couldn't trust anybody. Not outside of my brothers and Camy."

"That's a horrible way to live," she told him while her heart broke for the boy who'd felt so desolate and afraid that he'd make that type of resolution.

"Was it really? Because the minute I let my guard down again, Shannen jumped in, doing her dance about selling drugs to help her grandmother and using me to save her from Renaldo. That night of the raid I realized she'd been playing us both, sleeping with me and giving me tidbits of information on Renaldo's operation, and still sleeping with him too, taking his money and finally tipping him off about the planned raid.

"That's how he got to her. Since she wasn't only still dealing for him, but sleeping with him too, all he'd had to do was text her and she went running. He slit her throat and stuffed my business card in her hand to let everybody know he knew she was an informant. Then he came to the club and shot up the place just as our officers were going in."

In those moments Rylan was filled with a deep sorrow and simmering rage, all swirling around her as she stared at this man she'd thought she knew so well. In the end, she hadn't known this side of Del at all. It occurred to her in those moments that while she remembered everything there was to know about the boy, the man was a totally different person.

"I don't know what to say now," she admitted.

He shook his head. "I told you, you didn't have to say

anything." He walked away then, moving behind the bar to pick up a bottle and carry it to the table where the candles were lit.

There was no other request from him, so the decision was totally hers. Rylan unzipped and removed her coat. She smoothed down the wrinkled t-shirt and jeans she'd hastily slipped on and walked to the table, taking the seat across from him. He removed the top from the bottle and poured Hennessey in two glasses.

"I figured we might need more than your spiked hot chocolate tonight."

She didn't argue with him but picked up the glass he'd set in front of her right after he picked up his. "You figured right."

They sat like that for who knew how long, sipping from their glasses and looking at each other.

"I love you," he said after a while. "I think I knew it that morning when the sheriff told me your father was the one who pointed him in my direction."

Her heart did a stop-thud-stop-thud motion with his admission. "You had a very distressing way of showing that when you arrived at the shop."

He took another drink from his glass and nodded. "You're right. I had two gut punches delivered simultaneously. But you're right, I fucked up."

Was this the point where she told him she loved him too? Still. Because she'd really been trying to convince herself in this past week to toss that feeling out the door, unfortunately, it hadn't listened.

"I'm sorry for speaking to you the way I did and for not trusting you. But mostly I'm sorry for not believing in us, in what we had together. I don't know why I couldn't see it before that moment."

"Because you couldn't trust that you deserved something so good," she said. "Truth be told, I didn't trust it either. If I had I would've left the shop and come pounding on your door to tell you how much of an ass you were being. But I didn't." She shrugged. "I just walked away."

"I don't blame you."

"I did my part and you did yours," she said easily.

"Man, you're making this apology really hard with all this understanding. I was prepared to listen to you cursing me out."

She grinned. "Yeah, that's why you were adamant that I didn't have to say anything."

He tossed his head back and laughed.

"But seriously, I don't want to argue with you, Del. I meant what I said about us being adults. We both did what we did because we wanted to, I can own up to that. I didn't expect it to turn out like this, but it did."

"I didn't expect to fall in love with you," he told her.

She lifted her glass to her lips, took another sip and put it down. Then she waited a beat before saying, "I didn't expect to fall in love with you either.

New Year's Day

Del: Tell me what you like.

    Rylan: I like hot chocolate and morning wake-up kisses.

    Del: I miss the spiked hot chocolate.

    Rylan: You know where to find it.

    Del: So it's still there for me?

    Rylan: If the morning wake-up kisses are still there for me.

Del had been walking while he texted. A dangerous stunt considering this place was packed with guests of Ethan and Portia's wedding reception. They'd spent the morning at the Pleasant Rose Baptist Church watching as two people who hadn't planned on love but were smart enough not to let it get away, committed the rest of their lives to each other.

Del had always been the captain of the brothers. Yet today, Ethan had been their leader. He'd shown each of them that there was hope for a happy ever after if they just had the guts to reach for it. If there were ever a point in his life that Del had to gather up the courage to do something, this was it. He wasn't certain of the outcome, nor was he considering all the ways this could possibly blow up in his face. All he knew was that he'd been miserable all those days without Rylan and in the past four days since they'd been talking again, he'd known he didn't want to go through that trauma again.

He came to a stop behind where Rylan stood near the window by the back door. He'd seen her there as he'd walked down the stairs from the Skybox and had immediately taken out his phone to communicate with her—the same way he'd looked forward to chatting with her every night in the beginning, and the way they'd been doing this last few days since that night at the bar

"I'm still here for you, Rylan," Del said when he was close enough to her that he could smell the soft floral scent of her perfume.

She turned slowly and Del once again admired her in the short black dress that matched the other bridesmaids that had walked down the aisle this morning. He loved the way the top of the dress crisscrossed over her shoulder and hugged her breasts and torso, flared out at the waist and stopped just above her knees. The design left her long legs bare, the high-heeled shoes she wore giving him too many ideas of how he'd like to see her walking toward him wearing nothing else. But more than how sexy the dress made Rylan look, Del was also amazed by the light in her eyes as she'd smiled when she'd stood at the altar and the confidence that radiated from her.

Rylan wasn't like most women, because she was her own woman. She had her own mind and opinions and never failed to express them. So, if a man messed up with her, it was likely because he hadn't been paying attention. Del could admit that he'd been that guy.

"Are you sure about that?" she asked, clutching her phone in her hand.

"I'm sure about wanting, no needing you, more than I've ever needed anything else in my life," he admitted.

Del closed the small space between them. He reached out to take her free hand in his. He'd missed this simple contact. The warmth and comfort that had only come when he was with her. It moved through his body stilling the nervousness that he'd been trying valiantly to hide when he'd decided to approach her.

Music had started to play, the easy melody of a slow song. Anthony Hamilton, no, classic Luther and Del slipped his hands around her waist. It was the first time he'd touched her since their late-night conversation at the bar.

All they'd done that night was talk, until the sun had come up and they were both stunned that they were still sitting there. In the days that followed last minute preparations for the wedding had taken precedence and things had picked up again at the bar, so they'd been reduced to just texting. It seemed fitting that they'd get back to where they'd started, having conversations about each other's day but also delving deeper into what they each wanted out of life and out of a relationship.

She'd told him she wanted to find forever with someone and he'd confessed to never having that dream. But today as they'd all stood at the altar watching Ethan and Portia commit to each other, Del had begun to think differently.

"I like dancing with you," he spoke when their bodies were close and his lips were near her ear.

"You hate dancing," she replied as they swayed to the music.

"That's why I said I like dancing *with you*. And only you."

She pulled back enough so that she could look up into his face. "I like dancing with you too."

He was about to say something else, to tell her he'd missed holding and feeling her, but a loud round of applause stopped him. They both looked around at the sound only to find that the brothers, Camy and Portia included were all clapping for them. Other guests probably weren't sure what was going on, but they began clapping too and when Lance lifted his glass of champagne in salute to them, Del resisted the urge to give his smirking brother the finger. Damn he loved that guy, he loved all of them and prayed they'd all continue to grow in love and success.

"Seems like we're stealing the show," she said keeping her smile in place.

But Del knew she was uncomfortable being in the spotlight. That was Naomi and Camy's thing, Rylan was content to stay in her own quiet lane while reaching every one of her goals and he loved that about her.

"Yeah, let's not give them anymore free entertainment. I'll go my way and you'll go yours." He stated before dipping his head quickly to drop a kiss on her very tempting lips, a total contradiction to his claim about free entertainment. "When this is over, we'll meet up again at my place."

She surprised him by taking another kiss, letting her lips linger over his longer this time. "We'll meet at my place," she whispered.

Del frowned. "Your bed's too small."

She nipped his bottom lip. "Who said we'd be using the bed?" With a playful wink she eased out of his arms and he watched her walk across the room with a sway to her ass and his heart in the palm of her hand.

G★ME
Changers

DRINK
RECIPES

RYLAN'S HOT CHOCOLATE

INGREDIENTS

- 3 cups milk
- 1 cup heavy cream
- ½ cup sugar
- ¼ cup unsweetened cocoa powder
- Kosher salt
- 6 ounces Ghirardelli semi sweet milk chocolate, chopped
- 1 teaspoon pure vanilla extract
- Hennessy
- Whipped cream for topping

PREPARATION

1. Combine the milk, heavy cream, sugar, cocoa powder and a pinch of salt in a medium saucepan. Cover over medium heat, whisking occasionally, until sugar and cocoa powder dissolve. Do not boil.

2. Whisk in half the chopped chocolate until melted. Add remaining chocolate until smooth. Remove from heat and whisk in vanilla and a splash of Hennessy.
3. Pour into mugs and top with whipped cream.

PINK PANTY DROPPER

A Pink Panty Dropper is a pretty-looking cocktail, but don't let looks fool you, it can be stronger than you might expect.

- 8-ounce glass
- Ice cubes
- 2 ounces vodka
- 1 ounce tequila
- 2 ounces beer
- 24 ounce can of pink lemonade concentrate
- Lemon slices
- Strawberry slices

PREPARATION

1. Add the Ice - Fill the glass with ice until it reaches almost to the rim.
2. Slowly pour in the vodka, tequila and beer.
3. Add pink lemonade - Pour in pink lemonade concentrate until the glass is full.

4. Add Lemon and/or Strawberry slices

TIPS

The Pink Panty Dropper makes a great party drink. If you're planning to serve it to a crowd, make a large quantity ahead of time (without ice) so that the flavors have a chance to fully mix.

CANDY CANE VODKA

INGREDIENTS

- 5 candy canes, broken into small pieces
- 2 cups plain vodka
- Hot chocolate, for serving (optional)
- Whipped cream, for serving (optional)
- Crushed candy canes, for serving (optional)

DIRECTIONS

1. Combine candy canes and vodka in a mason jar and shake. Chill in the refrigerator until the vodka is bright red and the candy has dissolved, about 4-5 hours.
2. Serve cold as a shot or stirred into hot chocolate. If the latter, garnish with whipped cream and crushed candy canes.

ALSO BY A.C. ARTHUR

OTHER CONTEMPORARY ROMANCE

The Donovan Series, Donovan Friends, & Donovan Dynasty books
(in reading order)

Book 1: LOVE ME LIKE NO OTHER

Book 2: A CINDERELLA AFFAIR

Donovan Friends #1: GUARDING HIS BODY

Book 3: DEFYING DESIRE

Book 4: FULL HOUSE SEDUCTION

Book 5: TOUCH OF FATE

Donovan Friends #2: SUMMER HEAT

Donovan Friends #3: WINTER KISSES

Book 6: HOLIDAY HEARTS

Book 7: DESIRE A DONOVAN

Book 8: SURRENDER TO A DONOVAN

Book 9: PLEASURED BY A DONOVAN

Book 10: HEART OF A DONOVAN

Donovan Friends #4: A CHRISTMAS WISH

part of the *Under The Mistletoe* Anthology

Donovan Friends #5: ALWAYS MY VALENTINE

Book 11: EMBRACED BY A DONOVAN

Book 12: WRAPPED IN A DONOVAN

Donovan Friends #6: ALWAYS IN MY HEART

The Carrington Chronicles

Book 1: WANTING YOU - Part One

Book 2: WANTING YOU - Part Two

Book 3: NEEDING YOU

Book 4: HAVING YOU

* * *

The Rumors Series

Book 1: RUMORS

Book 2: REVEALED

* * *

The Royal Weddings

Book 1: TO MARRY A PRINCE

Book 2: LOVING THE PRINCESS

Book 3: PRINCE EVER AFTER

Book 4: TAMING THE PRINCE

* * *

The Temptation Series

Book 1: ONE MISTLETOE WISH

Book 2: ONE UNFORGETTABLE KISS

Book 3: ONE PERFECT MOMENT

Book 4: ONE CHRISTMAS SONG

* * *

Fashion & Passion

Book 1: A PRIVATE AFFAIR

Book 2: AT YOUR SERVICE

* * *

OBJECT OF HIS DESIRE

UNCONDITIONAL

LOVE ME CAREFULLY

HEART OF THE PHOENIX

SECOND CHANCE, BABY

SING YOUR PLEASURE

DECADENT DREAMS

EVE OF PASSION

PARANORMAL ROMANCE

The Shadow Shifters (in reading order)

Book 1: TEMPTATION RISING

Book 2: SEDUCTION'S SHIFT

Book 3: PASSION'S PREY

* * *

The Damaged Hearts Series

(Shadow Shifters Spinoff)

Book 1: MINE TO CLAIM

Book 2: PART OF ME

Book 3: HUNGER FOR YOU

Book 1-3: DAMAGED HEARTS BOX SET

* * *

Book 4: SHIFTER'S CLAIM

Book 5: HUNGER'S MATE

Book 6: PRIMAL HEAT

Book 7: A LION'S HEART

Book 8: A COUGAR'S KISS

* * *

The Wolf Mates

The Alpha's Woman (Available as part of the GROWL Anthology and CLAIMED BY THE MATE VOL.1 Duology)

Her Perfect Mates (Available as part of the WILD Anthology and CLAIMED BY THE MATE VOL.2 Duology)

Bound to the Wolf (Available as part of the HUNGER Anthology and CLAIMED BY THE MATE VOL.3 Duology)

* * *

The Legion

Book 1: AWAKEN THE DRAGON

Book 2: CLAIM THE DRAGON

* * *

WICKED: The Desireable Witches

CONTEMPORARY SMALL TOWN ROMANCE (W/A LACEY BAKER)

The Sweetland Series

Book 1: HOMECOMING

Book 2: JUST LIKE HEAVEN

Book 3: SUMMER'S MOON

Book 4: CHRISTMAS IN SWEETLAND (coming soon)

* * *

A GINGERBREAD ROMANCE, novelization of the Hallmark
Channel Original Movie

YOUNG ADULT PARANORMAL (W/A ARTIST ARTHUR)

The Mystyx Series

Book 1: MANIFEST

Book 2: MYSTIFY

Book 3: MAYHEM

A Mystyx Novella: MUTINY

Book 4: MESMERIZE

* * *

Pretty Little Liars Kindle Worlds

THE STRONG SHALL SURVIVE

BE MY SWEETHEART

ABOUT THE AUTHOR

Stay in touch with A.C. on the web!

Be the first to know when A.C. Arthur's next book is available!
Follow her at BookBub to get an alert whenever
she has a new release, preorder, or discount!

Visit the "Contact" page on her website,
www.acarthur.net, to sign up for her monthly newsletter.

"Follow", "Friend" and/or "Like" her on Facebook, Twitter,
Pinterest, Instagram, Tumblr, and GoodReads.
You can also find A.C. on Book + Main Bites
(https://bookandmainbites.com/acarthur22/bites).

f facebook.com/ACBookLounge
🐦 twitter.com/ACArthur
📷 instagram.com/acarthurbooks
📌 pinterest.com/acarthur22
BB bookbub.com/profile/a-c-arthur
g goodreads.com/acarthur

Made in the USA
Middletown, DE
27 January 2021